Wings of the Dawn, Book 1

Captive Beneath the Bahamian Sky

Kristen Hogrefe

Wings of the Dawn, Book 1
Captive Beneath the Bahamian Sky
by Kristen Hogrefe

Printed in the United States of America

ISBN 9781612154206

Unless otherwise indicated, Bible quotations are taken from The King James Bible.

www.xulonpress.com

To Mom and Dad for their love and
encouragement;
To my brothers Joe and David for their
inspiration and advice;
To close friends and family for their support;
and
To my Savior Jesus Christ for being my
source of hope and strength.

"If I take the wings of the morning, and dwell in the
uttermost parts of the sea; Even there shall thy hand
lead me, and thy right hand shall hold me."

Psalm 139:9-10

Contents

❧

Chapter 1

Crossroads

T he windshield wipers smeared the morning dew across his line of vision as Neil DeWitt began driving down the uneven dirt road. It was still too dark for anyone to see him leave, and he preferred it that way.

He was dressed in a pair of faded blue jeans and a gray jacket, and his dirty blond hair was still damp from showering. He had crammed his possessions into an olive drab duffel bag and tossed it into the back seat. The cargo that had been entrusted to him was neatly wrapped inside a watertight fanny pack, now concealed underneath his jacket.

Its contents pushed uncomfortably into his gut, but he ignored it. His partner had offered to stow it away for safekeeping, but there was no one he would trust to hide it but himself.

And he knew exactly the place, a place where no one would ever look.

He had since reached a paved road. On a whim, he pulled into the grocery store on the corner.

Inside, he looked for a small bouquet of flowers, which wasn't hard to find. There was a neat little display of graduation balloons and flowers just as he walked through the entrance. He looked past the roses and carnations to a cluster of sunflowers. His stomach tightened as he reached for them.

Minutes later, he was back on the road. He passed the St. Vincent public high school where he had graduated. That had only been seven years ago, but for Neil, it was a different lifetime.

He pulled through the familiar black metal gates and past the sign that welcomed him to the West Chapel Cemetery.

The dew was still falling heavily as he parked his car and started his way down the path, past the aged oak trees and beyond the small lake.

He remembered the first time he had walked this path as a teenager. He had never felt such pain before, and yet he had never been able to cry.

By the time he reached his sister's stone marker, he felt seventeen again.

He had been her big brother. He had carried her on his shoulders so she wouldn't have to get her feet wet in muddy puddles, helped her with her multiplication tables, and even rescued her kitten when it got stuck in the drainage ditch.

She had been so small and so trusting of him. No matter which fight he had picked, no matter if they had both been punished for something that was really only his fault, her devotion to him never seemed to waver.

She loved the most when he had picked her the sunflowers that grew in the easement behind their house. She had called them sunbeams that fairies planted.

He told her that was nonsense. He had picked them for her anyway.

But he was not seventeen; he was twenty-five, and she was nothing more than a distant memory, a dream cut short by the accident of time.

He felt the sunflower bouquet in his hand and dropped it to the ground. Susan was not the reason he had come.

He removed the watertight fanny pack, which looked almost rectangular due to its contents. Then, he kneeled down, and using a small spade, pulled back the grass in front of the stone marker. Quickly, he dug a shallow hole in the ground, inserted the fanny pack, and buried it, laying the sod back in place.

His Blackberry buzzed, reminding him of the rendezvous he had in half an hour. He quickly unearthed the old flower holder, half buried beside the tombstone, and pushed it firmly into the ground above the freshly disturbed sod.

Standing up, he looked around to make sure no one was watching. But of course there was no one. The sun's first light was just beginning to appear.

Satisfied, he turned back to look at the small grave. Reaching down, he picked up the bouquet he had tossed aside and inserted it into the holder.

If anything, it was his way of apologizing to Susan for the man he had become.

———————————————

Four hours later and miles away, a young woman with expectant hazel eyes waited for the moment she had worked so hard to reach.

"Abigail Mercy Grant."

The speaker carefully pronounced each word as Abby walked across the outside platform, the wind pulling at her cap and gown. It was a humid, blustery Saturday in Belmont Springs, but most of the graduates were too excited to care.

With a smile on her suntanned face, Abby accepted her diploma, shook the principal's hand and headed toward the stairs. Another gust of wind swept over the stage, and the eighteen-year-old's hand flew to her cap, which was pinned precariously to her curly brown hair.

She looked back to see her twin brother Steven as he secured his diploma. His broad smile and gray/blue eyes met hers. The two had shared practically everything growing up together – sunburns, chicken pox, homework, rock collections, make-shift model rockets, and best friends.

"Go Steve! Go Abigail!" A voice shouted from the crowd where family and friends took turns between applauding and fanning themselves with the commencement bulletins.

Abby recognized Andrew's voice, for he was the only person she knew who always called her by her full name. As she reached her seat once more, she could hear him cheering with his brother Matt and her older brother Jimmy.

Andrew was one of Pastor Baxter's two boys, and Abby had known him since the third grade. Donald Baxter was a chaplain in the Air Force when her father Bruce Grant first met him, and they had kept in touch, even after Baxter had left the military to pastor a local church. Abby always thought of him as a kind, wise, and smiley man; she never understood how a pastor could have such sons – especially a boy like Andrew.

Throughout her childhood, he had always been yanking her hair or teasing her cat or stealing her choir book. They had fished together, fought together and capsized in a kayak together. If anyone was to blame for her being a tomboy, it was Andrew.

She caught a glimpse of the tall, lanky young man with tousled sandy brown hair and waved.

The speaker's voice pulled her attention forward as the rows of graduates found their seats. When they finally grew quiet, their school chaplain stepped toward the mic and addressed the group.

"Everything you know is about to change."

There was a pause before he continued, and Abby sneaked a note to Steve. "We did it."

He smiled, but his eyes were glued on the speaker.

"You've accomplished a great deal, and you are certainly a mighty fine group of young people. Today is a celebration of your life, but it is also a turning point. I want to applaud your hard work, but beyond that, I want to challenge you. There are a lot of changes in store for you. For one, you've spent most of your high school years with the young men and women sitting beside you. After today, you'll all be heading your separate ways."

Abby stole another look at her brother, as the speaker's words echoed in her mind. She knew that in just a few short days, he would be leaving for an internship out west, but it was just for the summer. Surely not all that much could change over a few short months.

She was planning to start up her old summer job at the agency where her uncle worked as a private investigator. The thought of Rick made her want to search the audience for his face. She hadn't seen him sitting with her parents, but he had promised her he would be here.

"…If I take the wings of the morning, and dwell in the uttermost parts of the sea; Even there shall thy hand lead me, and thy right hand shall hold me," the speaker was saying.

Abby tried to focus on the speaker again, pushing aside her thoughts of Rick.

"These are the kinds of things that don't change," the speaker was saying. "God's Word and His promises won't change depending on your circumstances. The question is will you let your circumstances change you?"

The following moments were a blur. There was a prayer, an announcement, and then she was moving her tassel to the right side of her cap.

The next instant, the sky above became a sea of black caps, which the wind picked up and carried beyond the group of graduates below.

Chapter 2

One Week Later

The light changed to yellow, and Abby stepped on the brakes. As she came to a complete stop, she glanced in the rear view mirror just in time to see another plane ascend into the clouds. Minutes earlier, she had watched her brother's take off.

Steven would be gone for at least a month – probably more. He had met and befriended an archeologist during a school-sponsored fossil float in western Florida last fall. When David Carlisle had offered him an internship this summer, he could not refuse.

Abby was happy for him, though slightly jealous. Steven had an opportunity to jumpstart his career, and she was stuck at an intersection facing a red light.

She had learned from her mom that Rick had called just before the graduation ceremony, saying he would not be able to make it. He had not given a reason but had used work as his excuse.

Abby had been wondering when he would call her – if not to explain, at least to talk about the job he had promised her. Last summer, she had merely been an intern. Though unpaid, she learned how to type out reports, take calls and assist wherever possible. She had worked so hard. The owner of the private firm, Reagan Drake, had said they would bring her on as a paid intern the following summer.

Monday, she received the call. Mr. Drake had a niece down for the summer, a niece who wanted a job.

Life was not fair.

So, before taking Steven to the airport, she had dropped off five applications for summer work. With nothing left to do, she headed for Aviation Missionary Group located on the airport's perimeter.

The old set of hangars with a small office did not look like much, but it had been one of her homes away from home. She had spent countless hours volunteering in the office, sorting mail or delivering lunches to her brothers and the Baxter boys. The small but efficient base for the grace-centered organization had long been an integral part of her family and the church youth group. Her dad had encouraged Jimmy, and later her twin brother and her, to volunteer at the organization that delivered supplies to missionaries in the Southern hemisphere. A love for aircraft ran in the family, and the siblings had always felt proud to have Dad drop them off at AMG before he flew out with the Air Force.

She unlatched the chain link fence leading to the hangars where Jimmy would probably be at work and deliberately avoided the office so she would not have to chitchat. She just wanted to see Jimmy.

"Hello!" she called into the large hangar after seeing a pair of dirty trousers working under one of the Douglas DC-3s. A head poked out from under the plane, revealing a mass of wavy brown hair and a wide boyish grin.

"Abigail, what are you doing here?" Andrew asked.

"I just dropped off Steve and thought I'd swing by."

"Perfect timing – We're kind of short today . . ."

"Actually, I was looking for Jimmy," Abby cut Andrew short. She had not planned to stay.

"I see, you don't want to get your hands dirty," he teased. "And I was thinking you could help me wash old *Wings*. I'm almost done here."

"I just want to talk to Jimmy," she insisted.

"I can't help you there," Andrew shrugged, his head disappearing again.

"Well, where is he?"

"I can't hear you."

Rolling her eyes, Abby marched toward the DC-3 and crouched under the wings so she could see him. "I said where is he?"

"Why ask me? You said you just wanted to talk to Jimmy," Andrew was enjoying himself hugely.

"Fiddlesticks," Abby muttered and turned to walk away. "I'll find him myself."

"Well have fun looking," he shrugged and pretended to engross himself in his work.

Abby paused and stared at him, waiting for an explanation.

"Don't you remember?" Andrew relented. "He and Matt left for Haiti this morning."

With a groan, Abby turned away, crossed her arms and stared out the hangar toward the airport as plane after plane lined up on the runway and took off.

Andrew stepped out from under the DC-3 and cleaned the smudges off his dark-framed glasses before gazing intently at the young woman he had known since childhood. Her curly brown hair hung just below her shoulders, and the breeze was brushing it into her face. She was wearing her favorite pair of faded blue jeans and the polo he had given her for her eighteenth birthday just last week.

Wiping his greasy hands onto his overcoat, he slowly stepped behind her.

"Hey, what's going on?"

"Nothing at all."

"That bad, huh?"

"Horrible," Abby said, not turning to face him. "Steven's gone, my friends are on missions trips or working full time, and I haven't even got a part time job."

"What about that part time receptionist act you did last summer at your uncle's agency? That wasn't so bad, was it?"

"His boss gave the job to his niece."

Andrew wisely decided to change the subject. "I thought you were driving to St. Vincent tomorrow to visit the campus you'll be attending next fall. And weren't you going to spend the weekend with some childhood friend? That's something, isn't it?"

"Yes, but I need a job so I can start saving money for books and such. Oh! And I don't even know what I want to do with college and what I want to major in. I have all these interests, and they just don't add up to anything. Mom and Dad are at work, and I just wanted to talk to Jimmy."

"Well, I may not be Jimmy, but I'm a good listener," Andrew said with a smile.

"I know. It's just that … Oh, never mind," Abby said and turned to face him. He looked at the frown on her face and her furrowed eyebrows and laughed.

"Hey, I'm a captive audience if you'll help me wash old *Wings*," Andrew grinned.

"Why *Wings*? She hasn't flown since I was just a kid," Abby said.

"Well, I think I can add a few more years to her," Andrew said. "Besides, I've pretty much finished with the prep work on this plane for tomorrow's flight, so I thought I'd take a 'break' and give *Wings* a face lift. What do you say to that?"

Abby glanced at her watch but knew she had no place to be and nothing really to do but pack an overnight bag for tomorrow. With a sigh and a pretend huff, she allowed a faint smile to tug at the corners of her mouth.

"Hand me a spare pair of coveralls, and you have yourself a bargain."

"That's more like it," Andrew said and tossed her an old pair. "Just let me finish up here. You can go grab the hose and suds. I'll meet you outside where she's parked."

With a nod like that of a child sent on an all-important chore, Abby obeyed. Andrew was busy at the shop counter and still putting away his tools by the time she had everything. Glancing at the hatch door, Abby climbed the stairs leading up to the hatch and could not resist the urge to take a peek inside.

A hard yank did the trick, and she soon found herself standing in the dim interior. The air hung like a canopy about her and a dank, dusty smell filled her senses, but it was a flood of memories that overwhelmed her. This had been the first plane that she had stepped foot into as a child.

Her Mom had driven the then fifteen-year-old Jimmy to AMG to help out for the afternoon. He had been helping the pilots scrub one of the planes for the next flight, and Michelle Grant could not refuse him when he asked if Steven and Abby could take a look. The three had rushed off to explore the plane's interior and cockpit and play all sorts of imagination games as to destinations unknown.

Wings of the Dawn, the flight crew at AMG had called her. She had been a gift to the non-profit organization at a time when other planes were experiencing mechanical problems and had arrived just in time to meet a supply deadline. Though she was hardly a new bird, she was at the time a Godsend, the result of much waiting and prayer.

Now, she had been out of commission since the acquisition of some newer craft and sat at the corner of the property, as if parked for good. But the two

Baxter boys and Jimmy still held hopes that she would fly again.

"There you are," a voice from behind startled her. It was Andrew. "I thought I had specified we were washing down the *outside* of ol' *Wings*?"

"Sorry, I couldn't resist," Abby said, climbing out.

"Well, maybe you can help me out when we start doing some detail-work on the inside," Andrew grinned. "Kim and Amber Marshall volunteered to help, but if you want the job . . ."

"Nice try," she smiled, "but I hope by then to have myself a real summer job."

— — — — — — — — — — — — — —

Abby had packed a small bag that night and started first thing Friday morning for St. Vincent, on the opposite coast. She reached the university just in time to meet with her advisor, and now, what seemed like hours later, she was able to step outside into the sunshine and let out a big sigh. Being cooped up in Darcy Jordan's office had seemed like an eternity as the well-meaning woman inquired into her interests, plans for the future and goals. The interview had seemed frustrating for Ms. Jordan and herself alike.

Yes, she liked science.

No, she was not a huge fan of philosophy.

Just because she did debate in high school did not mean she wanted to join the college team.

No, she was not interested in joining the wind-surfing club.

No, she did not know what she wanted to do with her college education. She just wanted to be listed as an Undecided or a General Studies major for now.

With another sigh, Abby glanced down at her phone. One missed call, and it was Dixie. She and Dixie had first met in kindergarten and attended the same elementary school before Abby moved to Belmont Springs. Since then, they had been pen pals on and off through high school and had seen each other every once in a while.

Still, it had been three years since she had actually gotten together with Dixie. However, when Dixie learned that Abby was coming back to St. Vincent for college, she was thrilled, because she too would be attending the university. So when Abby told her she had a meeting with her new advisor, Dixie had insisted she spend the weekend with her.

Maybe it was the three years of never seeing each other. Maybe it was because she was feeling low on account of her recent interview with Ms. Jordan. Maybe it was neither. But regardless, Abby did not feel like spending the weekend with Dixie. She felt like driving home, moping a bit, petting her cat Sneakers, and hoping someone had called offering her a job.

And her memory of Dixie didn't seem too compatible with this sentiment. Dixie had always been bubbly, vivacious and spontaneous. Though not unintelligent, she had no common sense – like the time she spilled bleach on her favorite pink pajama pants. Instead of accepting the scientific fact that once bleached, bleached forever, Dixie applied every imaginable cleaning product to erase the "stain." That is, until her Mom explained that bleach is a cleaning product – a permanent cleaning product – that other cleaning products cannot outdo. The association of being outdone by someone or something clicked with Dixie, and she eventually reconciled herself.

Just that attitude made Abby wince at the thought of confessing her discouragement to her long-time, long-distance friend.

Still, Abby had not seen her in years, and this was an opportunity after all. She pulled into her driveway and glimpsed a glint of gold in the upstairs window. Before she had parked her car and pulled out the key, her friend had thrust open the door and bounded toward her.

Blue eyes sparkling and platinum blond curly hair bouncing, she embraced Abby in a bear hug the minute she stepped onto the pavement.

"I've been waiting hours and hours for you," she simply gushed. "My, how you've grown! But I guess we're both grown up now. Wait till I show you just everything. I'm so glad we can catch up! There's so much to do – we can go to the beach, go shopping. And you have to tell me everything. My letters are just awful; I don't know how you put up with them, but I'm much more interesting in person."

"I'm glad to see you too," Abby smiled, her resentment fading away. Dixie had not changed, and in a way, she was glad. Her friend had already managed to lift her spirits with her warm welcome.

"Let's get your things inside. Are you hungry? It's almost noon. Well, tell you what, I know this absolutely darling place called Sandwich Chef, so maybe we'll go there."

"Sounds good," Abby said.

"But would you mind if we stop at my grandfather's on the way? I promised I'd check on him. You see, his companion or nurse or housekeeper or whatever she does is off for the next two weeks, and I'm to look after him although he's asked me not to fuss. He tells me he can take care of himself."

"You mean Mr. Pennsbrooke, your grandpa?"

"Yes! Surely you remember Duff or Grandpa or Mr. Pennsbrooke – although that does sound awfully stuffy."

"Sure I remember him," Abby grinned. "He used to take us to that candy store when your mom took us to his place to play."

"His place is so huge it's enchanting although I can't imagine living there all by myself. I'd be absolutely creeped at night."

"Well anyway, I'll be glad to see him again. I wonder if he'll remember me," Abby said.

"You! How could anyone forget about you? Oh I'm so thrilled you'll be coming back to St. Vincent for college. It'll be like old times, won't it?"

"I hope so. It seems like only yesterday I waved goodbye. The years just go so fast."

"Dragged by is more like it. Why after you left, I thought the world would swallow me up from being bored until Henry came around. He's so darling. But well, he's put our relationship on temporary probation, so it's been boring."

Abby had heard enough about Henry in Dixie's rambling letters and wanted to avoid the subject if at all possible. It sounded to her that Dixie's Father– not Henry – had put their relationship on probation, and from the sound of things, she hoped it would turn into a more permanent estrangement. But Dixie had set her heart on many young men since she had known her, and she decided that one more heartbreak would be easy to overcome.

Their talk turned to different things as they drove toward Dixie's grandfather's place. Soon, Dixie wanted to know everything about Abby – her major, her plans. With a sigh, Abby briefly recounted her morning's academic meeting and admitted that she really did not know what she wanted to do with her future.

Her friend brightened on that topic. Dixie had only recently set aside her aspirations for nursing school and had decided upon a more modest course: secretarial science. She came to the conclusion that sticking people with needles just would not be as romantic as Grey's Anatomy presented it.

"But what about this summer?" Dixie asked suddenly, as they approached their destination. "What are your plans?"

Plans. Abby murmured to herself.

"What did you say?"

"Oh, my plans," Abby sighed. "The whole lot of them includes a trip to St. Vincent, a trip to see you, and a trip back home to find a job."

"Where at?"

Abby was about to make a rather dry remark, but they had just pulled into the Pennsbrooke driveway and Dixie had parked and swung open the car door. Abby followed her up the steps to the front door, where Dixie gave the ringer a solid push, causing the bell to echo throughout the rather large two story brick home.

"Gramps is going to be so happy to see you again," Dixie gushed and gave the bell another try.

And another.

"I can't imagine what's taking him so long," she frowned.

"Do you have a key?"

"I always forget about that," she said, peering into her purse and rummaging around. "It's just not like him not to answer.

"There we are," she said, twisting the handle and letting herself in.

"Gramps! Gramps! I'm here!"

"Mr. Pennsbrooke?" Abby hesitated.

"Oh, he won't like that," Dixie whispered. "Call him Uncle Gramps like you used to."

Abby smiled at the memory.

A faint sound upstairs drew their attention, and they raced toward it, taking the steps by twos.

"This way," Dixie said, heading toward the library. She swung the door open the rest of the way, drew forward and gasped, "Gramps!"

The elderly gentlemen lay sprawled on the floor, clutching his back and wearing a faint, peaked smile on his face.

"My little angel," he whispered, relief flooding his hoarse voice.

"Oh Gramps, how long have you been here?" Dixie said, falling to her knees to try to prop him up.

"Be careful, Dixie," Abby said, putting a gentle, but restraining, hand on Dixie's shoulder. "We don't know where he might be hurt. I think it would be better to call for help than try to move him ourselves."

"Where's the number?" Dixie asked.

"Probably on the fridge," Abby said, rising to her feet. "I'll find it. You go get him some water."

"Okay," she hesitated, not wanting to leave.

"He's not going anywhere, Dixie, but we need to hurry," Abby said and turned to hurry down the stairs. Dixie followed.

An hour later, Duff was comfortably propped up in his favorite Lazy-Boy downstairs, heat on his back and some faint color on his cheeks. Dixie sat beside him, holding his hand and scolding him for trying to reach a book that was too high for him.

The doctor turned to Abby as he headed for the door. "He needs around the clock care and watching," he said seriously. "He's strained his back pretty badly, and it will need time to heal. In the meantime, he has to take things extremely easy. I recommend you get a nurse to come every other day for checking his vitals, helping with bathing, etc. Here's a number I recommend.

"But other than that, he just needs care." He looked at Dixie. "A lot of her love, and a lot of your common sense."

"Thank you, Dr. Mack," Abby smiled. "I appreciate your getting here on such short notice."

"Duff's an old friend of mine," his eyes twinkled. "Take good care of him."

After closing the door behind the doctor, Abby returned to the den, which had since been converted into Duff's living quarters. He would not be climbing the stairs to his usual room any time soon.

What Abby saw made her smile. Duff was sound asleep, and Dixie was in a constant state of fussing about and making as much noise as usual while trying not to make any noise at all.

"Dixie," Abby whispered, waving her away from Duff. "Come here."

"I have to watch him," Dixie replied, walking toward her.

"He's not going to sneak out on you," Abby grinned. "He'll be fine; he just needs rest. But we need to talk."

"About what?" Dixie asked. Abby put a finger to her lips and nodded toward the living room where they wouldn't have to whisper.

"Who's going to take care of him and give him constant attention?" Abby asked. "You said his regular housekeeper is away for how long? A week?"

"The next two weeks," Dixie corrected.

"And in the meantime, someone is going to need to do more than just pop in on occasion. Duff can't cook, clean or take care of himself at this point. Now Dr. Mack gave me the number of someone you can call to come in every other day to check vitals, progress, and assist in bathing; but who's going to stay here to take care of him?"

"I hadn't thought of that," Dixie admitted.

"What's your parent's schedule look like?"

"Mom and Dad both have full time jobs. They could check in on evenings, but that doesn't solve the problem."

"What's your schedule like? I haven't even had a chance to ask if you have a summer job."

"I've done some babysitting here and there, but nothing definite," Dixie admitted. "I was kind of thinking I'd take the summer off."

"Hmm, well, then you're a prime candidate for looking after Duff," Abby said.

"Me! I couldn't – not by myself. I – I wouldn't know what to do or where to begin!"

"Well, you can cook …"

"Not really a fan," Dixie interrupted.

"Laundry?"

"Only when I have to."

"Cleaning?"

"We have a maid who helps around the house."

"I see," Abby sighed. "Well then, this is going to be quite the learning experience for you."

Dixie looked about her and sighed. The house had always seemed so still. It was far too quiet in her estimation – too quiet for her imagination to be left alone – even with Duff.

"Maybe you could stay with me," Dixie hesitated. "You said that you were still looking for a job back home, and well, I know Duff would pay you to help care for him. What if we both stayed here to watch over him, and that way, we could each get out every so often. And in the evenings, my parents could come over, and we could hang out together. Wouldn't that be sweet?"

"I don't know, Dixie," Abby replied. "I'm glad to help out for the weekend, but I really do need to get a job back home."

"Well, here's a job in a place that used to be your home," Dixie pointed out. "Wouldn't you like to spend some time here, getting reacquainted with the town? After all, you're going to be back in the fall for college."

Duff's voice from the den interrupted their discussion.

"Gramps, you're awake!" Dixie squealed, rushing to his side.

"You have a loud voice, young lady," he forced a smile. "It's easy to wake up a light sleeper."

"Oh, Gramps, I'm sorry. I'll be quieter next time."

"I heard what you were saying," he said softly. "I hate to be a burden to anyone, but I'm not too proud to know when to ask for help.

"And Abby, I would make good on Dixie's offer if you could stay here. I'd be more than happy to compensate both of you girls to stay here till Norma comes back. If you could look into that part time nurse, I'm sure the three of us could make it along just fine."

It would be kind of fun, keeping house, Abby thought to herself. Still, she hesitated. Somehow getting back home as soon as possible seemed the best way for her to take charge of her summer. She could follow-up on her applications. Maybe apply elsewhere. Just do something.

And yet, here was a place she was needed. She hadn't asked for this to happen. It just had. A little voice inside Abby reminded her that nothing happens by accident.

"If my parents give me permission, I'll be happy to stay the two weeks and be of whatever help I can be," she said, taking a deep breath.

"Hurrah!" Dixie cheered. "Now that that's settled, why don't you make all the phone calls you need to, Abby, and I'll go get all three of us some lunch at Sandwich Chef."

Dixie whisked her purse off the couch, swung it over her shoulder and skipped out the front door. Duff could only chuckle.

"I'm afraid Dixie doesn't think of 'playing house' as more than a game," he said.

Abby laughed. "If I were a gambling person, I'd wager that between the two of us, we'll make a housekeeper out of that girl yet."

"All things are possible with God," Duff conceded with a smile.

Chapter 3

An Uninvited Guest

Abby let herself sink into one of Duff's old Lazy Boy chairs and flipped open a copy of *Pride & Prejudice*. Though her finger stood poised at chapter one, her eyes wandered around the room. For the first time all day, she could take in everything that had happened: Duff's fall, Dixie's plan, her parent's permission to stay, arrangements for nursing care, housework, meal preparations.

It was just like playing house but for real. This time, there were no "papa" and no "mama" and no "baby"; it was just the three of them: a dear old grandpa, his loving but not very helpful granddaughter, and her.

She would be wearing more pink than usual. Dixie and she were about the same size, and her friend had happily volunteered to share her wardrobe, which consisted mostly of pink.

Abby's eyes fell upon the family portrait above the fireplace mantle. A very young Duff held a strong, secure arm around a young woman with a gentle, loving smile. Kneeling beside her were two young children, a boy and a girl. The boy was Dixie's father and the girl, the woman she once called Aunt. Duff hadn't wanted to talk about her, and Abby didn't pry. Thanks to Dixie, she hadn't needed to.

"She was really pretty," Dixie had begun her story. "I was just a little girl when she died – about a year before you moved away to Belmont Springs. But I remember her – and my cousins. Did you ever meet them? I think you did that one time. It was my seventh birthday, and my cousin Neil upset the punch all over us girls. Let's see, there was Mindy, you, Ashlee, Courtney . . ."

Abby had remembered the punch – and the stains in her dress that her mom was never able to remove.

"Anyway," Dixie had continued, "We – my cousins and I – used to play at Gramps' place together before the accident. Everything seemed so simple then.

"Dad never liked the guy his sister ended up with, and Gramps certainly didn't approve."

"Why not?" Abby had asked.

"Well, I didn't like him, because he always smelt like smoke. They didn't like him, because he had a record. Dad never mentioned him after Susan died."

"Susan was your aunt?"

"No, she was my cousin and about my age. Her brother Neil was about seven years our senior. We did lots of things together – before the accident."

"What happened?"

"Susan was accidentally poisoned or something like that. The police were unable to pinpoint exactly what happened, because no one seemed to know. The ruling was parental negligence, and her father went to prison for a spell. Her mom, my Aunt Sarah, never got over Susan's death. She died 8 months later."

"What about your other cousin?"

"Neil was about eighteen at the time and had been in and out of trouble at school. I really haven't seen him since, except once at his Dad's funeral last year. He didn't look at all like the boy who used to play hide and seek with me in Duff's backyard."

The grandfather clock in the living room struck 9 p.m. and startled Abby from her thoughts. She could hear Dixie watching TV upstairs and knew that Duff was probably asleep. Just in case, she decided to peek into his room to make sure he was resting comfortably.

Laying aside the book she hadn't even started, Abby rose to her feet and tiptoed across the room to the den. The sound of deep, heavy breathing met her ears, and she quietly closed the door the rest of the way. He should be fine for the night.

Yawning, she crossed the room back to the Lazy Boy. She was surprised at herself. Usually, she could stay up to midnight without a problem, but tonight, she felt she might have to turn in early.

"Just a few chapters," she mumbled to herself, curling up in the burly old chair. Chapter one left her eyes feeling weighted down. She started plowing through chapter two . . .

A sound startled her. Blinking open her eyes, Abby pulled herself up from her cramped position. She had fallen asleep with her head leaning over her right arm, and now she felt stiff.

It was a knocking noise. At first, she thought it might be Duff, but it was coming from the front door.

Dixie's television was still on, and Abby guessed she had also fallen asleep. The grandfather chimed 10 p.m., and Abby told herself she must have been dreaming.

But then came that knocking – more insistently – and Abby, now wide-awake, knew it was coming from the front door.

She slid out of the recliner chair, unconsciously dropping the book to the floor, and hesitated. With a frown, she glanced down at the yellow and pink ducky pajama pants Dixie had loaned her and pulled the short pink bathrobe tighter. She was in no mood to answer the door in such array and instinctively crouched low to peek out the large front window. The floodlight had since burned out, so all she could discern from the light of the yellowish lamppost was the outline of a man with some kind of bag at his feet.

Decidedly, she was not going to answer that door. Backing away from the window, she slowly crawled into the chair and waited, holding her breath that he would just go away.

He didn't. This time, he knocked so loudly she was sure he would wake up Duff.

Springing to her feet, she wanted to shush this unwelcome guest, but she had no intention of letting him in. Then, remembering that the kitchen overlooked the front entrance, she hurried there to crank the window open a notch, realizing to her satisfaction that he would have a terrible time trying to shimmy up the wall and break in through that route.

With a harsh shriek, the window budged, causing both herself and the stranger to jump. She fought the urge to duck out of sight.

"You there, what do you want?" she asked, trying to steady her voice. She could now discern that the man was in his mid to late twenties and had a tall, athletic build.

"Who are you?" he asked roughly.

"I think the question is who are you – and why are you calling at such an hour?" Abby was surprised at her own boldness and hoped she came across as stern.

The man squinted up at her, trying to make out why a teenager with a smart mouth was talking to him. He had expected a cranky housekeeper, not this girl-woman.

"Is this no longer the Pennsbrooke residence?" He tried to contain his agitation.

"And who wants to know?" Abby shot back.

"Relation to the family," he retorted. "Now I'm not going to ask again: Is this the Pennsbrooke residence?"

"Yes," Abby replied reluctantly.

"Is Mr. Pennsbrooke at home?"

"The nerve!" Abby muttered to herself. Aloud, she said, "Yes, Mr. Pennsbrooke is home, but he is not accepting visitors at this hour. You may try again tomorrow." She started to crank the window shut, but not in time to block out his smug reply.

"What grandfather do you know who would leave his grandson out in the night air?" His voice sounded self-assured, cool and faintly conceited.

Abby was speechless. She wanted to fire back a retort, but what if he were telling the truth?

"Wait there," she said, barely audible. The only person who could tell if he were really Duff's grandson was probably sound asleep upstairs. And she was going to have to wake her.

Sure enough, Dixie lay softly snoring on the guest bed, the TV turned low and some Doris Day movie playing in the background. Abby managed to find the remote to turn off the screen, and the lack of noise seemed to disturb her friend's slumber.

"Oh wake up," Abby kneeled on the bed beside her, gently shaking her.

"Go away," Dixie muttered. "I'm dreaming."

"Get up! There's a man at the door who claims to be your cousin," Abby said. "And I suspect he'll try breaking the door down if we don't get a few things straight."

Her words took a moment to sink in, but Dixie reluctantly agreed to put her feet on the floor and follow Abby to the door.

"What a sight we two make," Abby thought and couldn't help but smile at the humor of it. Dixie's curls were a mass of tangles on her head, and she had traces of mascara smeared under her eyelids. Abby didn't have to look in the mirror to imagine how ridiculous she looked in pink.

The banging on the door began again, which helped jar Dixie from her trance-like state. At Abby's coaxing, she looked through the peephole and nearly fell backward after one glance.

"It's Neil!" she exclaimed, more to herself than to Abby. "What on earth is he doing here?"

Before Abby could stop her, she had unbolted the door and swung it wide open. Abby stood at her shoulder, watching the scene before her unfold and not knowing what to do or how to prevent it.

"Well, Dixie, if it isn't my dear cousin!" Neil's tone changed from sarcastic to what sounded like sincere relief.

Glancing behind her to Abby, his smile turned into a crooked grin. "And here I thought I was being scrutinized by some watch hound. It looks more like I'm interrupting a girl's slumber party."

Abby blushed and knew he was enjoying what appeared to be the upper hand.

"Well, Girls, don't let me interrupt. I just have business to talk over with Gramps." He helped himself through the doorway and stood poised in the hallway. Dixie was about to show him in the rest of the way, but Abby stepped in front of him.

He looked down at the young woman and couldn't help but smile. Who was she to stand in his way? And yet, she was harmless, so Neil thought best to play along.

The patient, half-smiling look on his face made Abby cringe, but she stood her ground. "Girl's slumber party or not, Mr. Pennsbrooke has retired for the evening and is not to be disturbed."

"I'm sure he'd say differently if he knew I were here," Neil replied, tossing his jacket over the sofa. He slid his leather bag between his black-boot-clad feet and rolled up his sleeves as if about to dig into a day's work – or take out an opponent.

"I really just wish you'd come back tomorrow," she blurted out, while eying his jacket. There was a symbol on the sleeve that looked something like a cat's paw.

"And who exactly are you?" he asked. "Some long lost cousin of mine?"

"Abby's a friend of mine," Dixie chimed in. "She's promised to stay here to help take care of Duff until his regular housekeeper returns from a vacation. It's very good of her."

"Yes, very."

"You've met before," Dixie continued. "Remember my seventh birthday party?"

"Not really," Neil's patience was wearing thin.

"But that brings us to you, Mr. . . . ."

"DeWitt. But call me Neil."

"Well, Neil, what exactly are you doing here?" Abby asked.

"Does a grandson need an excuse to dote upon his grandfather?"

"Doting is reserved for business hours, evenings around the fire, and weekend trips," Abby reminded him. "Not quarter to eleven."

"Traffic, what can I say?" Neil yawned. "Look, are you going to make me wait here all hours of the night to see him?"

"He's not well, Neil," Dixie said. "He had a nasty fall today and needs his rest."

"That's too bad."

"Perhaps tomorrow morning you can see him," Dixie offered. "I just don't want to wake him."

"Quite right, of course," Neil hurried to agree. "Well, you girls head off to bed, and I'll make myself cozy in the living room."

Abby had no intention of being shooed off to bed and quickly disagreed. "Oh, the living room is no place for a grandson to stay," Abby said. "Here, I'll clear my things out of the guest room upstairs, and you can stay there. I'll camp out here."

"No need to inconvenience yourself on my account."

"Oh, I don't care. I like camping. And besides, this way I can hear Duff if he needs anything. I'm a light sleeper, you know."

"Really," Neil forced a smile.

Abby was back in a flash with her overnight duffle and pillow. She smiled disarmingly at Neil as Dixie eagerly showed him upstairs. In their absence, she managed to move the couch so that it blocked nearly any possible entrance to Duff's room. Satisfied, she tucked in a couple sheets, found a quilt, and tossed her pillow in place.

She retraced her steps to the front door to make sure it was securely bolted before returning to the living room where she caught Neil DeWitt quietly slipping down the stairs.

"Looking for something?" she asked from behind him. To her satisfaction, he jumped.

"Um, the um, kitchen. I was thirsty."

"Well, help yourself to the fridge," Abby said with polite hospitality.

"I will."

"I'll wait to turn out the light so you can find your way back up the stairs," she called after him.

"The brat," he muttered to himself. He rummaged around in the kitchen for a cup, settled for a glass of water, and returned.

Abby stood waiting at the hallway that connected the stairs, living room and kitchen, as if guarding the light switch. She made no attempt at small talk as he headed for the stairs, her silence implying he was nothing more than a naughty child who required supervision.

"Good night, Mr. DeWitt."

"Yes, well, good night," he said tersely. He watched as she turned off the light and disappeared into the living room, where he imagined her to curl up contently on the lumpy couch in front of Duff's doorway.

He remembered her all right. She had been at Dixie's party – one of the little girls he had intentionally spilt punch all over. It had served them right. They had been flitting around in their pretty little garden dresses, and he had felt they needed to be taken down a notch. Oh, they all cried to their mothers and pointed their fingers at Dixie's big mean cousin who had "accidentally" let the bowl slip when they were standing in front of it. All of them had whimpered and whined.

All of them but Abby. When everyone else had run away, she had stood in front of him, stared him down, and seen right through him.

Instead of running off like the rest of the children, she had taken the cup of punch in her hands and tossed it all over his shirt.

Two hours later, the house was still, dark and quiet. Two hours later, the guest room door slid open and a man silhouetted against the shadows softly slinked down the stairs, avoiding every creak that had been scrawled into his memory as a child and teenager. Finding his way to the kitchen, he gently slid open the door. It was the only door that didn't creak, as he recalled, and the years had not been that many since he was a teenager.

Securely gripping a bundle under his arms, he slipped into the night air. Not ten minutes later, he re-entered the door, hands empty, and easily made his way from the kitchen to the stairs. Neil paused at the edge of the living room, from where he could discern the rhythmic breathing of a deep sleeper.

"Bluffer," he smiled to himself. She would be easy enough to keep in the dark.

Chapter 4

A Spoiled Surprise

✵

Kim Marshall was dripping with soap-suddy water, and her old sneakers were half buried in mud, but she was smiling. She, her sister Amber, and Andrew had spent all afternoon and into the evening doing a detailed scrub of the old DC-3 – inside and out – and she was flushed with satisfaction. Andrew was still working on its mechanical makeover, but at a glance, the craft looked good as new.

Kim and Amber were the nieces of Ian Smitt, assistant manager, pilot, and general mechanic for Aviation Missionary Group. They had grown up with the Baxter brothers and Grant siblings, and the young people were virtually inseparable.

"I can't wait to see the look on Matt's face when he comes in tonight," Amber grinned. Jimmy and Matt were scheduled back from Haiti this evening, and both were "in the dark" as to the plans for "*Ol' Wings*" that Andrew had initiated.

Andrew smiled to himself. He knew Matt was interested in Amber. Now if only his other matchmaking efforts were so successful. He had often told Jimmy that Kim was an equally good catch, but his friend had always shied away from the idea. After all, Kim was Abby's age, and for all Andrew knew, Jimmy might just think of her as a sister.

The trio was just putting away their cleaning supplies for the evening when the familiar humming of a plane's engine filled the air. Sure enough, several moments later, they glimpsed the familiar AMG plane taxiing down the runway. The "pit crew," as Andrew jokingly called the AMG team's flight crew, set to action. Everyone, it seemed, had been awaiting the crew's return from Haiti, and Andrew watched the familiar scene unravel as he had many times before.

Yet something was missing. Just yesterday afternoon, Abby had been moping around, complaining she had no one to talk to with both her brothers away. That was Thursday. Today was Friday, and he had since received the voice message Abby had left on his phone. He must have been working on mechanics, because he had never heard it ring.

For a moment he let his eyes wander to the faded army-fatigue cover of his scratched cell phone and toyed with it between his fingers. Then, he dialed the voice mail button and hesitantly held the phone up to his ear.

"Hey, Andrew, it's Abby. Just wanted to call to let you know I won't be able to help with *Wings* for a while. Dixie's grandfather had a fall, and they've asked me to stay on and help out around his place. Might as well, I suppose, since I really didn't have anything to do back at Belmont. But I am glad you asked me to help you start cleaning *Wings* last night. It was fun, and well, thanks for being there. Tell Jimmy I'm sorry I missed him and punch that brother of yours in the shoulder for me. I'll catch you later."

There was a pause. Then the automated voice said, "To replay your message ... to save . . . to delete, press . . ."

"There you are!" Jimmy's voice boomed into the hangar, and Andrew nearly jumped. He slipped the phone into his pocket and walked forward to meet his friend.

"How was the trip?" he asked, slapping him on the back.

"It was kind of long, but well worth it, as always. We would have been back sooner if we hadn't had some delays. But where's the welcome committee?"

"What welcome committee?"

"That sister of mine," Jimmy grinned. "I figured she'd be hanging around here in Steven's absence, complaining of boredom."

"She's not in town, actually, and won't be back for a while. She went to St. Vincent, remember?" Andrew said and briefly relayed the story. At that moment, Kim and Amber appeared with Matt in tow.

"Hey Jimmy, they tell me they have a surprise waiting for us," he grinned.

"A welcome committee after all," Jimmy winked at Andrew. "We pilots have a lot to finish up here, but how about tomorrow morning? I'm coming in early to handle my paperwork, but I'll be free mid-morning to early afternoon."

"I don't get off work until noon," Amber said.

"Then let's plan on lunch, and you can tell us all about it," Matt said.

"What are you up to tomorrow, Andrew? Will you join us?"

"I'll be here," he said with a broad grin. "I wouldn't miss this surprise for anything." He gave Matt a solid slap on the shoulder, smiled to himself, and turned to help the flight crew prepare to roll the plane into its hangar.

————————————————

Bright and early Saturday morning, Ian Smitt's red pick-up drove into the empty lot belonging to AMG. Once parked, he jumped out and walked around to open the passenger door. A young woman clad in blue jean overalls hopped out and skipped to keep up with her uncle's long strides.

Neither spoke a word as the pilot unlocked the door and Kim posted the mail. The average onlooker might have wondered at their lack of conversation, but theirs was a relationship of understanding. Unlike most coworkers who routinely repeat the same idle comment or question to each other day after day – "Good morning, how are you?"– This pair could share silence, enjoy it, and communicate through a smile.

After tossing his jacket over the bulky, scratched – but clean – office chair, Ian Smitt walked around back to the hangars and planes, while Kim took a moment to organize her office space and projects. Her goal today was to send out the last three AMG monthly missionary letters, which were already printed and folded. The office was still hoping to purchase a stuffing machine, but until that day came, Kim and Amber stuffed and prepared mailings by hand.

She flipped on the radio, cleared off the conference table and set to work, alternately humming and singing. That was the beauty of working early and alone. No one was there – but her uncle – to interrupt her thoughts or work flow. And if Ian did hear her, he would only smile to himself and marvel at a girl who prefers working early to sleeping in late.

Amber was just like her, except her work commitments had extended to a part time shift at the local bookstore. She intended to go away to college next fall to study pre-medicine and had picked up extra jobs to offset the oncoming expenses. Kim still had one year of high school left and planned to remain as a part time office assistant at the mission while taking dual-enrollment classes in addition to her regular schoolwork.

Half way in the middle of whistling a tune, she paused. Her thoughts had drifted to Amber, who for the last three years had worked right beside her on Saturday mornings. Still stuffing envelopes at a steady pace, she glanced at their picture on the key chain of her office key. They had flown down to Haiti last summer with their uncle for a short "mission trip" sponsored by their church. Being only a year apart, she and Amber had practically done every-thing together their whole lives, and her not being there created a void.

Change. She was already beginning to sympa-thize with the restless spirit she had sensed in Abby a week prior to Steven's departure.

Two hours later, her hands slowed from their task, now just over half way done, and she glanced at the clock. Only a quarter past ten. If she kept at it, she should be finished before noon and before the others arrived. The last hour she had been imagining the look on Jimmy's face when he'd see old *Wings* looking almost new again.

Almost. Even Andrew's mechanical wizardry could not reverse the effects of time, but their efforts were impressive, and Kim was proud. And hopeful. That plane had been such a delight to all of them as children.

She arched her back and peeked at the clock. Only another minute had passed. Surely a five-minute break wouldn't upset her schedule. The mail-ings would still be done on time, and after all, she did need to stretch.

She pushed back her chair and rose to her feet. The radio hummed along, but above its buzz, she could hear her uncle at work in the second hangar. She knew he wouldn't mind if she stole a quick break, but still, she didn't want to have to explain her romantic sensibilities for the old DC-3.

Cracking open the door leading from the break room to the first hangar, she peeked inside. No one was in sight, but to her surprise, the hangar door was open. Assuming her uncle must have opened it, she hurried through its mouth to the edge of the property where *Wings* was parked.

Andrew had given her a spare key yesterday, so she had no problem letting herself inside. With a hard yank, she slid the heavy door aside and climbed in. She would only be a moment.

Just a few minutes before, a white pick-up had pulled around back, and a tall pilot wearing a checkered shirt had stepped out. His dark black hair was shaped to a short crew cut, and his otherwise attractive brown eyes furrowed to form a frown. His long fingers tapped his left wrist impatiently as he retraced his steps. Where had he lost his watch?

Jimmy hadn't planned to arrive at the mission before noon, but during the course of the morning, he discovered that he had left – or lost – his wristwatch the previous evening. It was not an expensive watch, but one of his Haitian friends had given it to him for a present last Christmas, and the gift itself meant much to him.

For a moment, he paused by the half-closed conference room door. Perhaps someone might have seen his watch and left it for one of the girls to find in the morning. But he could hear the radio humming and decided against interrupting. He didn't want to have to explain.

After taking a closer inspection of the hangar, Jimmy reluctantly turned toward his truck, empty-handed. A faint noise caught his attention, and he glanced at the old plane parked on the property's edge. His eyes widened at the opened cockpit door and instinctively, he took off running in the immediate direction. Perhaps the girls hadn't latched the door securely, and the wind had caught open the door.

Slowing as he neared the craft, he tilted his head to the side, listening for a noise. Soft footsteps faintly sounded from within, and he cautiously approached the open door.

"Hullo?" he called inside. "Is someone in here?"

The footsteps hesitated. Even more carefully, Jimmy proceeded to enter but stopped short. There, standing in front of him with her face twisted into a frustrated frown, was Kim, dusting cloth in hand.

"Kim! What on earth?" Jimmy started but stopped short at the sight of the neat, cleaned, and improved interior.

"It wasn't my idea," she began. "I mean, of course I helped, but oh, now you've spoiled – I've spoiled – everything. We've all worked so hard – I mean, Andrew, Abby, Amber, and I – to surprise you and Matt, and I just wanted to take one last look to put on, well, any final touches – and I didn't mean to be long. That's why we asked you both here for lunch, and we were all going to surprise you and have a great time of it. But now, I'm here, and now you're here, and our surprise is . . . is, well, ruined." Her lower lip puckered, and Jimmy thought she might cry.

"I don't know what to say," Jimmy rubbed his forehead, trying to take everything in. He certainly was surprised – stunned at the craft's condition. Never in a hundred years did he expect to see *Wings* return to her former glory.

One more look at Kim's soiled dust cloth and even more downcast expression knocked him back to reality.

"It's incredible," he managed lamely.

"But everyone's going to be so disappointed that you already know," she said.

"Well, they don't need to know that I already know," Jimmy smiled.

"What do you mean?"

"We could just pretend that I never discovered *Wings*, that I was just taking a walk around the perimeter, and that you just stepped out for a breath of fresh air. That conference room can get a little stuffy if you're cooped up in there for too long."

Kim managed a nervous chuckle as she thought over the scheme. It wasn't great, but it would have to do.

"I guess that will be fine," she said out loud, as if talking to herself. "If you really act surprised . . ."

"I will," Jimmy promised, smiling.

"Well, okay. But you'd better get going then."

"You first, Miss Marshall," Jimmy said.

Kim blushed and without another word, disappeared. Jimmy stood inside for a moment longer, taking in everything. After a minute or so, he stepped outside, locked the door behind him, and headed back to his truck, having completely forgotten about his watch.

Chapter 5

An Unsatisfied Snoop

❦

A beam of sunlight peaked through the living room curtains, falling across the couch and inching its way toward Abby's face. She had planned to be up before now but had forgotten to pack her alarm; her internal clock had stopped ticking the minute she hit her teenage years.

Her forehead began to crease, and her eyes tightly pressed shut as the light played across her eyelashes. With a pathetic groan, she rolled to her side to shut out the brightness – and in doing so, landed decidedly on the floor.

"Oh!" Her eyes shot open as her hands felt the cool, hardwood floor. Shaking her head, she blinked and finally took in the couch, floor and what she decided at the moment to be a most distasteful shade of yellow/gold on the living room curtains.

Yesterday came back to her. She remembered her trip to the "guidance counselor's" office at St.

Vincent University and its bland aftertaste, her reunion with Dixie . . . finding Duff on the library's floor, something about why she was sleeping on a couch . . . Neil!

Abby jumped to her feet and glanced reproachfully at the ludicrous pajamas she had borrowed from Dixie. The house was far too quiet for the sun to be up, and she wanted to go check on their late-night visitor.

But first, she glanced in at Duff, reproaching herself for being anything but a light sleeper. Had he called during the night? Did he need anything?

The mantel read 8:15 a.m., and she slipped through the door to get a better look. Duff's breathing was easy to detect, and its rhythmic quality assured her he was resting comfortably.

Creaking the door shut, she glanced about the room, which appeared undisturbed. Next, she peaked out the front window. No stork had delivered Mr. DeWitt, and she wanted to know what kind of car he drove.

"Hmm," she muttered to herself and stood up higher on her tiptoes to look out. She saw Dixie's car and her own, but no other vehicle was in sight.

"He didn't just walk here," she muttered, unconvinced. With a determined sigh, she started for the stairs and stopped at the guest room, ashamed of herself. What a snoop she was turning out to be!

"Uncle Rick always says never to do anything half-heartedly," she reminded herself. "It's all or nothing!" And with that, she leaned toward the door, listening for sounds.

Silence.

Her perplexity growing by the minute, she headed toward Dixie's room and waited a moment. She could certainly hear her friend's snoring!

Softly, she moved down the stairs, grabbed her overnight bag, and closed herself into the bathroom in the hall. A moment later, she emerged in jeans, a t-shirt, and sneakers and hurried to the kitchen to start coffee.

By the time coffee was brewed, it was 8:45, and no one besides a teenager or an elderly man had a right to be sleeping, in her estimation. Pouring a generous cup for herself, she sipped the hot vanilla flavoring and made her way once again to the stairs.

She boldly knocked on the guest door and cleared her throat.

There was no response.

She knocked louder and called a somewhat weaker, "Good morning?"

Still no response.

With a huff, she resorted to placing her coffee on the wood floor and kneeling down to peek under the doorframe. By squinting, she could make out that the comforter was an equal distance from the floor on all sides, that there were no shoes or slippers lying about and that the bag Neil had brought with him was nowhere to be seen. Finally, her eyes nearly crossing, she made out a slip of paper on the floor, inches in front of her face.

Gritting her teeth, she picked up her coffee and twisted the handle. The door sprung open to reveal the bed made, hangars neatly arranged in the closet, doilies still adorning the guest bureau, and note placed visibly on the wooden floor.

"Thank You."

Her nose wrinkled as she picked it up. Breaking the seal, she unfolded the page and read:

My Dear Hostesses,

You really have been most kind to put me up for the night. Sorry for what seemed to be a rude intrusion, but really, Gramps would have wanted to say hello.

As for Gramps, I'm sorry I have to run like this, but I have business elsewhere. Do thank him for the hospitality, and tell him I'll visit again soon.

And Abby (as I'm sure you will first read this), as you can see, it was quite unnecessary to give up your room. Next time, leave the couch to me. I was afraid I might wake you this morning, but as I discovered, you are not quite so light a sleeper as you thought.
Gratefully yours,
Neil

The very tone of the note nettled her. Ironic. Maybe sarcastic. He really didn't mean a thing he said.

"Dear hostesses, gratefully yours," she muttered to herself. What on earth was he up to?

A sound downstairs caught her ear, and she tossed the note onto the bed. Duff was awake, and now her morning would be occupied. But her mind would be elsewhere.

When Dixie finally descended the stairs at quarter to eleven, Abby had done the breakfast dishes, Duff's nurse had come and gone, and Duff now sat comfortably propped up in his favorite chair in the living room.

"Good morning, Everyone!" Dixie smiled a Cheshire cat grin before sprawling out onto the couch.

"A little late for good morning," Duff said. Turning to Abby, he said, "Dear, would you mind getting the paper? An old man needs some entertaining."

Abby smiled, playfully punched Dixie and headed outside. The humid air slapped her in the face, but she welcomed getting out of the house.

She still had not told him about Neil. For one, she wanted to make sure breakfast settled and he didn't give the nurse any trouble.

For two, she wanted to check with Dixie to make sure she hadn't dreamed up the whole thing.

Her thoughts elsewhere, she barely noticed the voice of a neighbor calling out to her.

"Hello there," the elderly woman said.

"Oh yes," Abby replied distractedly.

"I'll say, you've had a busy night – and busy morning," the lady whistled. "How is Mr. Pennsbrooke? That doctor arrived so late last night – and left so early this morning that I was genuinely alarmed.

"I thought to myself, that dear man can at least afford good care," the woman continued uninterrupted. "I told my John, there are doctors and then there are doctors.

"But I didn't realize it was a doctor at first," she paused.

"What do you mean?" Abby asked.

"You see, I didn't know it was a luxury sedan," she said. "I took one look at those darkly tinted windows and said to myself, Good Lord, it's a hearse!

"Then my John – he does seem to know everything – told me that it was nothing of the sort and just the kind of car a wealthy-to-do doctor might drive. He set my mind to rest. But I still don't understand why a doctor would want such a terribly dark tint on the windows . . ."

Abby managed to slip away from the dear busybody and delivered the paper without a word. It was Dixie's turn to play house. She was going to take a long hot shower . . . and let her mind wander to the sedan with the dark-tinted windows.

———————————————

They were all sitting on the back porch when Abby and Dixie finally decided to tell Duff about last night's visitor.

Tactful as ever, Dixie blurted out the story in one breath, leaving Duff speechless, confused, and rather agitated.

"Just like his dad. I don't like it," he kept saying over and over to himself. "Just like his dad. . .

"If he comes back, you come and tell me, even if I'm sleeping," Duff insisted.

They nodded and Duff fell silent. Abby wanted to ask questions, but now was apparently not the time. Dixie tried to ease Duff's mind by saying that Neil probably wouldn't return. He must have been low on cash and just needed a quick "hotel."

Abby wasn't as convinced. Neil had wanted to sleep on the couch – with Dixie and her neatly tucked away upstairs in bed. Why would he want free roam of the house if he hadn't wanted to see Duff? After all, he had left without even saying a hello or goodbye to him.

No, she was sure Neil would be back. And this time, she was determined to discover why.

Later that evening, after Duff had retired, she and Dixie were playing cards out back, watching the sunset. The day had been filled with the chores of housework and home care, and Dixie was already beginning to question if they were cut out for the job.

But Abby wasn't listening. "Dixie, tell me about Neil and your childhood together. What did Duff mean when he said he was just like his dad?"

"I don't know," she shrugged. "He was probably being general. Neil had a bully streak in him as a kid. When we played hide and seek here, he would chase us so hard we'd run crying to grandma, or he'd hide so well we could never find him.

"Still, he was soft on Susan, his little sister. She would always cry when he played rough with me. I don't know what's become of him. I mean, I'd see him so kind with Susan; and then, I would hear about the fights he'd get into at school and with his dad. I never knew what to make of it."

A gust of wind caught some of the cards on the table and tossed them onto the steps leading up to the porch.

"Bother, I'm tired of cards, Abby. Let's go inside before it rains and watch a movie or something to get our minds off everything."

"You go ahead," Abby said. "I'll be just a minute getting those cards." The daylight was dwindling fast, and Abby had just enough time to spot half a dozen of the stray cards scattered at the base of the porch steps.

She skipped down to collect them and retrieved all but one, which had half slipped through a cracked, slightly ajar board toward the end of the porch. When she reached to pull it out, a splinter slid right under her nail, and she immediately pulled back, wincing.

Some weekend this was shaping up to be – complete with a delinquent grandson, a spoiled granddaughter, and her, picking up after everyone and everything, even these worthless cards.

In frustration, she kicked back, her finger still smarting from the splinter. The wood gave way easier than she had thought, and she was alarmed to see she had kicked through a small hole.

But it wasn't just rotten wood. It went deeper. She bent down on her knees to feel for the card, and in doing so, her hand swept against the corner of a solid, square package. The light was gone and she could just barely touch the crinkly packaging.

Probably just some old trash, she thought to herself as she fell backward and rose to stretch. But then, she paused. There was a slight smell, a faint, but nevertheless sickly sweet, smell.

Dixie was calling to her, and she had retrieved all but that last card.

She called back, "Just one more minute!" Pressing her lips together, Abby bent down again, but out of the corner of her eye, she detected movement close beside her.

Turning half circle, she found herself staring into the face of Neil DeWitt.

He reached out toward her as if to yank her away, and she jumped back, bumping her head against the porch's edge.

"What are you doing?" The rage in his voice alarmed her.

"These cards . . ." she started, rubbing her head. "They scattered . . . What on earth is the matter?" His distorted face and glowering eyes frightened her.

"And what on earth are you doing here again?" She staggered to get her balance, as her head throbbed.

The porch door distinctly slammed shut, and Dixie appeared on the scene.

"Neil! What's wrong? Abby?"

Before she could react, Neil had grabbed her firmly by the arm and marched her up the stairs, his face masked with concern.

"Dixie, didn't you ever tell your friend about the rattlesnakes we had under the porch? I didn't mean to startle her, but I was afraid she'd find a nest.

"You are all right, then?" His eyes bored into hers, and Abby felt lightheaded.

"You surprised me so . . ."

"Is she okay? What's wrong with her head?" Dixie started chattering with excitement.

"She's fine; it's nothing a cool glass of water won't help," Neil directed Abby to the sofa. In the middle of things, Duff emerged, and the fabricated rattlesnake tale was retold as Abby was hushed into silence and ordered to recline on the couch.

Five minutes later, she could hear the muffled voices of Duff, Dixie, and Neil in the kitchen. All Abby could do was stare at the ceiling, trying to make sense of everything.

But when she closed her eyes, all she could see was the rage in Neil's eyes that had nothing to do with his recent concern about rattlesnakes.

———————————————

Abby did not argue about giving Neil the couch that evening. The conversation downstairs was dominated by what were, in her estimation, ridiculous fairly tales told convincingly by a man she was more and more growing to distrust and dislike. He had pooh-poohed her every time she tried to jump into the dialogue, and though she sensed Duff doubted his grandson's interests, he did not seem overly alarmed. With his prince-charming concern for her head "bump" and effusive flattery for Dixie's ability to make smores, Neil waylaid everyone's suspicions. Everyone's but Abby's.

To satisfy Duff's curiosity, he explained he had some business in the town opposite St. Vincent, but had wanted to stop by and say hello. It had been a long time, after all.

"I'll be gone tomorrow," he promised. "I'll be returning to my work in Miami . . ."

"And what exactly do you do, Mr. DeWitt?" Abby cut him off.

He smiled at her patronizingly, as one would smile at a child who pretends to understand politics.

"My dear Abby, I wouldn't trouble you with the boring details. To keep it simple, let's just say I'm an inside sales rep for a manufacturing firm."

"What is it you manufacture?"

"I don't manufacture anything," he laughed. "Must I explain the occupation of an inside salesman to you?

"At any rate," Neil resumed, his voice growing husky, "I thought I'd stop by West Chapel for old time's sake before leaving town for good."

The room fell suddenly silent, and Abby grew impatient. It seemed everyone knew exactly what he meant but her.

"What's in West Chapel?" she ventured at last.

"My sister's grave," he said.

"I'm sorry," she whispered. She excused herself on account of her "headache," which Neil had been playing up all evening, and retreated to her room. She could not stand to let herself feel sorry for a man she did not trust.

Closing the door behind her, she pulled her laptop and cell phone out from her bag, fluffed the pillows on her bed, propped them against the headboard, and quickly changed into her pajamas.

Abby didn't know exactly what she was looking for, but she wanted to know more about Neil DeWitt. She typed his name in her search engine, which brought up pages of "Neil DeWitts." Frowning, she tried narrowing by city. Other than finding his name listed on his school's football team, she didn't discover much about him.

Then she tried "Susan DeWitt," and a news article and obituary appeared. There was a picture of her by a garden of sunflowers taller than she was and next to her, a lanky youth. He was grinning from ear to ear as he pretended to measure his sister with a sunflower. Abby couldn't help but smile. Maybe she was all wrong. Maybe she was overly suspicious.

But then her thoughts wandered to the punch episode and her own close encounter this evening, and she shook her head. No, something wasn't right and hadn't been in his life since childhood. She was surprised at how well he could cover up the storm inside with a grin or compliments. He had been so smooth tonight, but she had caught him off guard earlier and looked into his eyes, which had momentarily betrayed some secret.

As she looked up the location of West Chapel Cemetery, she picked up her cell phone and dialed the familiar number. She knew it was getting late, but it could be later.

"Hullo? Who's this?" A groggy voice asked.

"Hey Andrew, it's Abby. Do you have a minute?"

"Do I what?

"Is now a good time for you?"

"A good time to sleep! Abigail Grant, have you looked at the clock? It's past eleven."

"Sorry, I have a mystery person, and I need someone to help think with me."

"Not again," Andrew muttered. "If this one is like the UPS man with the gimp, you can forget it."

"How many UPS men do you know who have gimps?" Abby retorted hotly. "They have such physically demanding jobs . . ."

"Don't start," Andrew moaned.

"Never mind then. I'll just deal with the up-to-no-good grandson myself. Good night!"

Abby flipped her phone shut and frowned. She hadn't wanted to argue, and now she was upset with herself for taking her frustration out on Andrew – but he had thrown the UPS man story in her face.

With a sigh, she looked at the West Chapel map on her screen. The cemetery was located off East Clairmont Street. But who was she to solve Neil DeWitt's mystery? And what business was it of hers?

Her phone chirped. It was Andrew.

"Look, Abigail, I'm sorry . . ."

"No, Andrew, I'm sorry," she interrupted. "It was thoughtless of me to call so late, and you're right, it's probably the fault of my overactive imagination anyway."

"Are you sure you don't need to talk?"

"Yeah. No big deal. I'll call you later."

Abby said goodnight, turned off her cell phone, shut down her laptop, and turned off her light. When she slid under her covers, she realized just how tired she was.

She had almost fallen asleep to the sound of raindrops spattering against her window when she heard a creaking noise. Abby started to toss off her covers but stopped herself, pressed her lips together, and lay back down. "It's just your imagination," she whispered to herself. "He'll be gone tomorrow and will never trouble you again."

Chapter 6

West Chapel Cemetery

A bby picked up two packages of bacon and frowned. She had no idea what her dad bought. Grocery shopping had always been her dad's duty, and if she happened along, she usually just pushed the cart.

But here she was, on a Sunday morning, in the local grocery store, because there was nothing in the pantry but canned beans, and Dixie had insisted that Duff looked forward to his housekeeper's Sunday morning breakfast.

So, instead of sleeping in until an hour before church, as was her routine back in Belmont Springs, she was delegated to errand girl.

It had been quarter after seven when Dixie had appeared in her nightgown, giving her the task before slipping back into bed. Duff was still asleep, and Neil, apparently gone again. Well, that was that.

She picked up a carton of eggs, a gallon of milk and headed to express. She was waiting in an unusually long line when her cell phone started to vibrate. Frowning, she balanced her items with one arm while opening her cell phone with her free hand.

"What's up?" she yawned into the phone. Dixie deserved to know how tired she was.

"Thank goodness you answered! We're all in an uproar!"

Abby was not overly alarmed. "If Duff's not well, all the numbers are on the refrigerator; and if you're not sure how to work the coffee machine, wait until I get there."

"It's Neil! Oh Abby, there are two cops here, and Duff is so distressed . . .

"What? But Neil was already gone by the time I left."

"That's just it . . . He's in trouble – or suspected of trouble. And now he's not here, and they're asking so many questions."

"Like what?"

"Like if he were using Duff's home for a cover-up – What an outrageous idea! – to stow away himself – or something else. They – the police – won't say exactly, but Duff's getting himself all worked up, and Abby, just come home as quickly as you can!"

Listening to Dixie and juggling her goods was not working well for Abby, who accidentally bumped into a flower display at the end of the express aisle.

"Hey, watch it!" the man behind her said.

"Sorry!" Abby whispered, trying to set the flowers back to their upright position. "Hey Dixie, I've got to go. I'll be home as soon as I can."

Her hand grasped the cluster of flowers. Sunflowers.

"Hey, I've got an idea. Talk to you soon!" With that, Abby hung up, set her articles on the conveyor, and selected the sunflower bouquet. She had a hunch, and there was no time to think it through.

After checking out, she ran to her car, tossed the food in her backseat, and began driving away.

"East Clairmont Street," she murmured to herself, craning her neck to catch the street signs. She was a little rusty on the roads, but the general way of things had not changed much since she was a girl.

She spotted the candy store. What child would forget it?

"Now I'm sure the cemetery was around here," she said to herself. "I thought there used to be one down the street from the candy store . . ."

There it was. East Clairmont Street. The West Chapel Cemetery.

She parked her car, grabbed the bouquet, swung open her door, and paused. The large graveyard spanned at least five acres with a lake, chapel, and hundreds of tombstones. She hadn't the faintest idea where to look.

And she suddenly felt nervous. What if she were right? What if Neil had hidden something at his sister's grave?

An old grounds worker was planting some flowers near the entrance, and she hesitantly approached him.

"Excuse me; I'm looking for a grave marker."

"There's an index in the chapel with the layout of the plots," he replied, his wrinkles forming a smile.

"Thanks," she said and hurried down the sidewalk. Inside the small chapel, she easily found the index and scanned the pages. Dabner, Dawson, Delaney, DeRosa, DeWitt. . .

Her breath caught as she read the names of Sarah and Susan DeWitt. Mother and daughter.

Their graves were right by the lake. She clutched the flowers a little tighter and with a determined step, left the chapel behind and began walking down the mulched lane. Tall oaks graced the water's edge, and some ducks were busy with their morning bath.

Time. She glanced at her watch. It was only half past seven, yet she knew Dixie would be waiting for her and probably be in a tizzy by now. She knew she did not have time to enjoy the scenery.

After glancing at several monuments and headstones, she finally found the one – or two. Susan's was right next to her mother's, and both rested beneath one of the old majestic oaks.

Falling to the ground, she pulled away some weeds from Susan's headstone and read the inscription: Susan Hope DeWitt: our little sunflower of hope on earth.

A tear slipped down her cheek. She couldn't help it, for the thought occurred to her how different life might be for some if these two graves had not yet been dug.

Her hand laid down the sunflowers and in doing so, felt an object half buried in the ground. The rain last night must have eroded away some of the earth that covered it. Digging deeper, she managed to unearth what looked like a black fanny pack. She pulled back the zipper to reveal a small brown package inside.

A faint symbol on the packaging caught her eye. The symbol was of a paw print, similar to that of a cat's; yet it was unusual, because its claws were extended, and a cat's claws are never extended, except in a fight. She had seen it somewhere before.

The cocoon of plastic zip-lock bags finally gave way to reveal a lightweight, porous "brick."

A pungent, sickly sweet smell stung her nose as she fingered the substance. Where had she smelt that before?

Her mind spun as the pieces fell into place. The cards, the wind, that package, Neil's rage, the storm, Dixie's call, the gravestone, the sunflowers . . .

The sunflowers. She glanced to her left where she had dropped them . . . but they were no longer there.

Never did she hear the man who had sneaked up behind her, with cat-like agility. Blackness engulfed her, as if a curtain had fallen over her face and blocked out the sun.

She fought a claustrophobic fear as she tried to find her way out of the tarp or bag that now obstructed her vision. Her arms floundered at someone who kept trying to grab her.

And then the world below her gave way as her feet struck a hard, knobby object, catapulting her forward. She felt the skin of her palms peel back on the oak's old roots that lay exposed, eroded above the surface.

A whooshing sound seemed inches away from her ear, and she stumbled blindly back to her feet, one hand finally catching the outer edge of the bag on her head.

With a hard jerk, her arm tossed aside the bag, and she gasped for fresh air. For just a moment, she detected a man's silhouette to her left. But her eyes, so recently blackened, had not fully adjusted to the sun's brightness, for spots now played across her vision.

She knew he was running toward her, and she tried to shake the daze that seemed to cling to her very being. Her head pounded, but she forced her legs to action, only to find herself once again tumbling into a heap on the ground.

She could hear the sound of his approaching footsteps and grasped for something to defend herself with. Her hand brushed against an object, which her mind registered as the trampled sunflower bouquet. Desperately, she threw it at his face but not in time.

A sharp pain. Blackness. She collapsed onto the ground, swept into unconsciousness, as the yellow petals floated away in the breeze.

— — — — — — — — — — — — —

A damp chill, a dull ache, a gentle hand. Someone was pulling her, dragging her, easing her up an incline. Mud oozed between her legs; long blades of grass slithered past her sides; mustiness clung to her nostrils. A chill jarred her body into a shiver, but she couldn't tell if the cold were real or just a sensation from a dream. Maybe if she could pull her covers higher above her head she would be warm.

Her head. It rocked back and forth. She was in a rocking chair. Her head throbbed as the chair rocked faster and faster. She would fly off the chair soon. She needed to stop the chair. She couldn't stop the chair.

She was falling. Her hands grasped at the ground, the grass, the mud. She couldn't stop herself. The shadows were darkening. She couldn't see. All she could hear was a roar, a distant roar.

It was like an angry ocean crashing against a cliff. A wail, a long cry.

A voice. Or was it the wind? A whisper. A prayer.

A man's voice. "Wake up, wake up!"

So she was dreaming after all. She would just wake up from this dream, this very strange and painful dream.

"Come on, open your eyes. You poor thing."

The sun's morning rays nearly blinded her as she peaked out from under her eyelashes. A blurry form started to take shape. Old overalls, a bearded face, a wrinkly smile, anxious old eyes.

"You are there after all," he whispered. "You poor thing."

It was the old gardener she had met earlier that day, no, not minutes before. Before what?

Abby tried to think but couldn't. She leaned into the man, who was cradling her head.

Her feet were damp, wet, and cold. She was wet all over. Wet and muddy and achy.

She couldn't think. It hurt too badly. The sun burned her eyes, and she fell backward into the man's chest, which seemed to give way to an abyss, and she just kept falling.

———————————————————

Dixie had no nails left to chew. The police had questioned Duff and her up and down, sideways and forwards. If someone had asked her to multiply or divide 100 by 2, she would have cried.

Where was Abby? She had called over an hour ago. She should have been back forty-five minutes ago.

And then the police wanted to know where Abby was. Dixie had called her cell phone time and time again and received no response.

The police searched the house, the yard – the entire neighborhood it seemed. Dixie explained that she and Duff had no idea what Neil was doing in town. He had said his trip was business related, and he had seemed rather harmless.

Duff had nearly collapsed after the police accused Neil of hiding himself – or something else – at his place. Dixie wanted to know exactly what they meant, but she never received any definite answer.

Abby would know what to say. She would also know which doctor to call for Duff who was beside himself that Abby had not appeared.

As she sat staring out the window where police were still sweeping the lawns, her cell phone chirped. She snatched it up off the table and flipped it open.

"Hello?"

"Is this Dixie?" a woman's voice trembled.

"Yes, who is this?"

"This is Michelle Grant, Abby's mom. I just received a call from St. Vincent Hospital about Abby."

"Where is she? What is it?"

"She's at the hospital with a concussion and is in and out of consciousness. The nurse said she was clubbed in the head. Oh, Dixie, what is going on? I don't understand. I thought she was taking care of Duff. What happened?"

"She just went out to buy groceries this morning. She was supposed to be coming right back. I had no idea . . ."

"We're on our way, but we won't be there for a couple hours. Can you check up on her? Be with her?" Mrs. Grant's voice cracked.

"Of course, sure," Dixie said in a daze and jotted down the room number and information.

When she hung up, she found an officer waiting at the doorway. Before the man had a chance to speak, Dixie blurted out, "I have to go to the hospital. My friend's hurt."

"Do you think it's related to DeWitt?" he asked, gently.

Dixie hadn't even thought about Neil. Could he be responsible? "She's been clubbed – I don't know what happened. I just need to be there," was all she said and excused herself.

The ten minutes it took Dixie to arrange for a neighbor to stay with Duff, provide a coherent statement to the police, and grab her purse seemed like an eternity. When she finally found herself staring at the starched, white hallway that led to room 305, she felt transported to a different world. An hour ago, she was still asleep in her bed.

A nurse met her at the door.

"I'm her friend. She was staying with me," she whispered, her throat suddenly dry.

"Second bed, closest to the window," the nurse said.

"Is she …"

"She's conscious, but resting. I'd let her be. The doctor will be in shortly."

Dixie nodded and turned to approach the bed where Abby lay. Her head was lightly bandaged, while her body was cocooned in a layer of white sheets. White. Starch. So impersonal. So unfamiliar. So painful.

Dixie wasn't sure how long she stood there before the doctor appeared. "She's suffered minor head trauma," he began, as if reciting a prescription from a medical textbook. "Her concussion does not seem severe, and I see no reason she won't be as good as new within three weeks. All she needs is lots of monitoring and rest.

"A police officer is waiting at the front desk. I believe he wants to ask you some questions for his report."

"A police report?"

"Yes, of the accident – er, incident."

"What happened?"

"That's for you and the case officer to discuss. This way, please."

Dixie accepted his arm and walked out the room, casting one last glance back. Three weeks, good as new.

If only she could bandage the day and make it all better. But Dixie had a feeling that a bandage might only cover – and unsuccessfully at that – a much larger problem.

— — — — — — — — — — — — — —

The evening sky was fading into shades of light pink and yellow so that with the white curtains pulled, a soft glow filled the room. Mrs. Grant and Dixie had left half an hour before to check up on Duff and grab something to eat, but he had stayed. They had been at the hospital two hours, but Abby remained asleep. The doctors assured them she was doing well – The medications were probably contributing to her drowsiness. He wasn't quite convinced, and he wanted to hear her story.

And knowing Abby, she would want to know the rest of the story – everything that had unfolded since that blow.

A faint sunbeam played across her face, and he detected her nose wrinkle, her eyelids flutter. Finally.

Her world was fuzzy at first. The room gradually came into focus, and Abby became aware of the white walls, hospital smell – hospital food smell, even worse.

Staring down at her – was that her Dad? He was hard to make out – almost as if she were staring up into the sky, but from under the water.

"Dad?" She was surprised by her own voice. So unsteady, unsure.

"I think the doctors had better lighten up on that medication. Don't try to sit up – you'll get a splitting headache. Just relax, and give yourself a minute."

The voice was most definitely not her father's. "Andrew?"

"That's more like it!" He was grinning now – She could tell by the way his voice rose.

"What's going on?"

"You're in the hospital with a concussion," he said gently. "Do you remember what happened?"

"What happened?" Abby thought to herself. She pressed her head against the pillow and detected a dull ache. She must be medicated, or else that dullness would be intense. She had been in a cemetery. There were sunflowers. She had been going to see Susan's grave. Dixie had called. She hadn't said where she was going or why. Maybe she wasn't sure herself or didn't want to have to explain a sudden impulse.

She wasn't sure what she had expected to find, but she had found something. Yes, it was a package of sorts.

What had happened then?

She blinked her eyes open, and this time, her world was in focus. She was definitely in a hospital. Was Neil responsible for this?

"How bad am I?" she managed, wanting to feel her head.

"Doctor says you'll be as good as new in three weeks," Andrew said cheerfully, almost too cheerfully.

"Tell me honestly," Abby said firmly. "Am I really all right?"

"Doctor's prognosis looks promising," Andrew said, "but as to whether you were ever entirely sound before entering the hospital, well, that's a little less certain."

"Very funny."

"But seriously, you should be fine. You just need lots of rest."

"Hmm, well, can you tell me what happened?"

"You first – if you remember. I'll pick it up from there."

"I remember going to the cemetery. I found the grave or graves I was looking for, and then I found something else. It was all wrapped up in plastic bags and hidden just below the surface by the tombstone. I wasn't sure what it was, but it seemed important. And then, I don't remember anything. It's like looking back into a fog." Abby looked apologetically up at Andrew. She detected displeasure on his face.

"Don't you think you were a little rash?" he scolded.

"I don't know – I don't even know what I expected to find. I was looking for something. It was an impulse."

"An impulse?"

"Yes, and stop with that look on your face. I found something anyway."

"You did?"

"Yes, it was a package of sorts and had a sickly sweet smell. I'd smelt it before."

"And that's what someone clubbed you over the head for?"

"Is that what happened?"

"Well, someone whacked you over the head, picked you up, and tossed you in the nearby lake. You're lucky you just landed in the marsh – and face up."

"I don't believe in luck," Abby corrected.

"You know what I mean," Andrew said. "Anyway, a groundsman found you shortly afterwards and called for help."

"Did he see anyone?

"He didn't say that he saw anyone although another man did come by and help him with you."

"I wish I'd seen his face. Could it have been Neil? Who else? I wonder if he really meant to kill me," Abby frowned.

"Well, clubbing someone over the head isn't exactly a gesture of friendship."

"Oh, enough of the sarcasm, but really, I wonder," Abby's voice trailed off. "It must be terribly important."

"What?"

"That package. I've got to find out why."

"Oh no, you don't," Andrew said. "You're on bed rest for three weeks."

"Oh, please, I feel better already," she insisted, trying to sit up. An intense pain jarred her head, sending her falling backwards into her pillow, eyes tight from the pain, voice gasping.

"Wooh, take it easy," Andrew eased her back into a comfortable position.

"Maybe I'll take a week or two off," Abby managed humbly. "And by the way, why exactly are you here?"

"Is that some new expression of gratitude?" Andrew asked.

"No, I'm really glad you're here – I mean, of course, it's good to see you – but I just wondered, why you?"

"Well, your mom and Dixie are both here as well. They just stepped out for a moment – they'll be back soon. Your dad is traveling on business this weekend, so I offered to drive over with your mom. Jimmy had another flight to prepare for, and of course, Steven's out in Texas. Your mom even tried that uncle of yours . . . I'm kind of your last option."

"Well, thanks," Abby smiled, reaching for his hand. She softly squeezed it and closed her eyes, smiling to herself. "I feel so tired – Will you wake me up when Mom gets here? I want to see her."

"I suppose – but you need your rest."

"Yes, Doctor," she said, her eyelids once again heavy.

"That's more like it," he grinned and squeezed her hand back.

"But only for three weeks," she squinted back at him.

"Go to sleep," he scolded her. He hoped that three weeks would be enough time for this Neil character to skirt the country and go backpacking in Africa, Asia – anywhere – just so that Abby would never have to meet him again.

Chapter 7

Setbacks

Neil stared out into the street and waited. Sheets of rain fell from the Bahamian sky, pelting the palm trees and sending small children running barefoot home through the mud. He could just imagine the look on their mothers' faces as the tramps muddied the floor.

He glanced down at his watch and wiped off the fogged-up face. It was a quarter past nine o'clock. Where was Kurt?

The last two weeks flashed through his mind. They had been so close to delivering the first shipment. Months, years of preparation and cost weighed in the balance.

This was more than their regular clientele asked for. Those shipments were merely mercenary, for funding. This was so much bigger. Endless possibilities. Mind-boggling ramifications.

Promotion. Prestige. Profit. He had all but tasted them, dreamed of the leverage they would have with the world's black markets. Manipulation. Manpower. Money. It made the rotten world go round.

And then this. When they least expected, someone had slipped.

And not just someone. It was Zachary Ocho. Did he just get sloppy? No, that word never defined his vocabulary. Did his luck run out? Never had Neil seen him lose a bet or see a venture turn sour.

Not like this. Not when it mattered so much.

Not the man who taught him what he knew, made him who he was.

Not Zachary Ocho.

A jeep skidded to a halt in the mud as the monsoon-like weather persisted. Neil lifted his jacket above his head and ran out to meet his partner, slamming the door behind him.

"Have you heard the latest?" Kurt asked, shifting to reverse.

"What's the word?"

"Our men have salvaged the shipment. Just in time too. We barely slipped under the noses of those hounds, but we made it. Of course, we're back to square one as far as setting up the exchange and reassuring our client that next time, there will be no risks involved. It sets us back a few weeks, maybe months . . ."

"What do you know about Ocho?" Neil interrupted.

There was a pause. The only sound was the rain pounding upon the glass and the windshield wipers swooshing. The jeep felt dank. The air hung like a canopy.

"He's out, Neil. Done with. For good."

"Just like that?"

Kurt cleared his throat. "Yeah, the word is he just slipped up. There was some kind of accident earlier today. Of course."

"Of course," Neil said.

"Some say Keegan will take his place."

"Zarchoff won't pick Keegan, and you know it. He's too entrenched in African diplomacy. He doesn't know the South American angle. Not like Ocho did. Not like I do.

"That's why you came to see me after all, isn't it? You came to take me to Zarchoff to get my new orders."

Kurt cleared his throat again. "You know, Neil, just following orders."

"The day you stop repeating that cop-out line is the day you'll have your own assignment." Neil swore. Not at Kurt, just at life.

"Maybe I like just following orders. You don't have accidents."

"Right. Like Peters. Jayden. Now Ocho."

They drove in silence. The road was full of pot-holes, and Neil could hear the mud slosh against the tires. It would be half an hour before they would reach the airport and an hour after that before they would land – in this weather.

Neil closed his eyes, and in his mind, he was already there ... walking down the halls, barking orders at the guards, cursing at the natives who maintained the grounds and not for a small fee – not a small vow of silence. There were accidents if that vow was broken.

Accidents. Kurt slammed on his brakes to avoid a rut in the road, sending mud splashing onto the windshield. Neil blinked back in time to another so-called accident, not so long ago.

The papers had spelled out the story just as their man had fed it to the press: Girl assaulted in cemetery suffered concussion. Lack of concrete evidence left police unable to verify attacker or confirm rumored tale of local trafficking. Grandson once suspected was cleared of all culpability.

He had even ordered flowers to be delivered to the hospital for the victim, sending his best wishes for speedy recovery.

He had sent sunflowers. His jaw twitched, but he soon regained composure.

After all, accidents were part of life, the normal rhythm of life's ebb and flow. Life was an accident, so Ocho once said.

———————————————

The last stamp licked, the last envelope sealed, the last label peeled ... until tomorrow. Abby stretched, stared out the window and sighed. She was back to where she had started: restless, without a job – without a paying job, that is, for she did stay busy three days a week, six hours a day volunteering at the AMG office.

All she had earned so far this summer was a generous check from Duff for helping Dixie for three short days, a concussion, a trip to the hospital, and three long, boring weeks of bed rest.

Duff's regular housekeeper had cut her vacation short to return to his care, and Dixie had spent most of her time texting Abby. What a sensation, what a stir. They had filled out the report, Abby had made her statement, the police buzzed about the business for a day or two, and then, absolutely nothing came of it.

The verdict was unpremeditated assault by an unknown person.

Had she actually seen Neil or recognized his voice? Did she have any concrete evidence to identify him as her attacker?

All she had was a hunch, a very strong hunch, and her suspicions.

Who, other than Neil, would have a motive? What about the package?

"Ah, yes, the package," Abby thought ruefully. It was conveniently missing from the crime scene.

It was probably just a figment of her concussive disorientation.

Of course, the case detective had attentively listened to her story, her suspicions. He had kindly assured her they would keep looking for her assaulter. Since she had no known enemies, he surmised it was a random, unpremeditated attack by an intoxicated tramp.

It just seemed too convenient, too coincidental.

A soft knock on the conference room door made her look up. It was Andrew. He smiled and looked down at the two cans of soda in his greasy hands.

"I needed a break and thought you might too," he grinned, handing her a cola.

"Thanks," Abby said. "I've just finished up though. I thought I'd head out a little early. Steven's coming home tonight you know."

"Yeah, we're all coming over for dinner. Your mom's too good to us."

Abby chuckled. She knew her mom was as excited as she was to have Steven home and would probably make more food than they could eat.

She sipped her cola and sighed. "Steven's going to have so many stories to tell."

Andrew almost choked on his drink. "As if you don't have your own story to tell," he said.

"It's not the same," Abby said. "He's moving forward in his career. All I got was a bump on the head, a trip to the hospital and three weeks of bed rest."

Andrew paused. "Abby, sometimes God uses things we would never have chosen for ourselves to bring us where he wants us to be."

"Is licking envelopes and pasting postage your definition of the center of God's will?" Abby looked doubtful.

"Hey, look at me," Andrew said. "You know how much I wanted to be a pilot. Ever since I was a kid, I wanted to fly planes and join the Air Force like your dad.

"And then I hit my teenager years, and my vision went south. It seemed like every year, the eye doctor kept bumping up the strength of my prescription glasses and dashing my every hope to be a pilot."

"But you like what you do," Abby said.

"I do now," Andrew corrected. "When Ian offered to teach me mechanics, I hated the idea. But I did it, because my dream was gone, and I didn't know what else to do with myself."

Abby toyed with her empty can. She had heard Andrew's story before, but what did it have to do with her?

"But do you know what I've learned from Ian – what I've learned from working on *Wings* these last few months? Do you know what I realized, Abigail?"

Her head shot up at the sound of her full name. It sounded so strange sometimes, since everyone else just called her Abby.

"I realized that without mechanics, we couldn't have airplanes. And without airplanes, we wouldn't have pilots, and we wouldn't be able to send the supplies our missionaries need."

"I know, Andrew," Abby said and rose to leave. "I'm glad you like what you do. I'll see you later tonight – and thanks for the cola."

"Sure, anytime," Andrew said as she disappeared from sight. He sighed to himself, "I wonder if she heard a word I said."

He closed the door to the conference room behind him and slipped inside the hangar where Jimmy was working.

"You just missed Abby," Jimmy said.

"We were actually just talking," he said.

Jimmy looked at his friend. "Do you think she's okay? She still seems awfully quiet."

"I don't know," Andrew shrugged. "She doesn't seem very happy, and she doesn't seem to understand what it takes to be happy."

Jimmy smiled. "God has his way of teaching each of us what we need to learn."

Andrew sighed. "Well apparently, he's going to have to whack her over the head with something stronger than a two-by-four to get her attention."

Jimmy laughed. "Don't wish another concussion on my sister, please."

They worked a couple moments in silence before Jimmy spoke again. "What do you make of the problem Ian's been having with the Cessna?"

"He said it might be about due for an engine overhaul. We're hoping the problem isn't that extensive."

Jimmy whistled. "That would take a while and put us short. Are you working with him tomorrow?"

Andrew nodded. "We're coming in early to diagnose the problem. I'm kind of hoping his first suspicion is wrong."

"Ian's rarely wrong, you know."

"I know," Andrew said. "It's just that the N700 DC-3 is coming up for routine maintenance. With the Cessna out, we'd be running a skeleton force. And we have two flights scheduled for next week: one to Port-au-Prince and one to Nassau."

"Can you service the N700 early?" Jimmy asked.

"I've asked for time off with Steve back in town, but you know me; I'll come in if I need to," Andrew grinned as his brother Matt walked towards them.

"We should all get together, once that brother of mine's had a chance to get settled," Jimmy said. "I hear he's been flying all over the States with his archeologist friend."

"Count me in," Matt said. "Mind if I invite a couple friends?"

"I don't catch your meaning," Jimmy said.

"The Marshall girls, of course," Matt said. "Kim and Steven always got along just fine."

"Kim and Steven?" Jimmy asked.

"Those girls are growing up, in case you haven't noticed. They're not just Ian's cute little nieces."

"I know," Jimmy turned to look away. Maybe he just took the girls for granted, but he had never thought Steven liked Kim.

He knew Matt and Amber were good friends, but Kim was just his sweet little helper. Or wasn't she so little any more?

"Of course, ask them along," was all he said.

— — — — — — — — — — — — — —

Abby pulled her car door shut, yanked at her seat belt, and reached into her purse. As she stuck the keys in the ignition, she flipped open her cell phone and read "one missed call."

She blinked in surprise. It was her uncle's office number. Why was he calling her? She dialed voice-mail and listened. "Hi, Abby, it's Rick. Sorry it's been a while, but you know, busy as usual. Give me a call when you get this. Bye."

She frowned. It really had been a long time since she had seen her uncle – or even talked to him. He had been on an assignment and missed both her birthday and graduation. In fact, she realized that she hadn't seen him since Easter when she had begged him to come with her family to church for her choir's cantata.

With a sigh, she hit the redial button and pulled the keys out of the ignition. Talking to Rick and driving would not be the safest of combinations.

"Drake and Benton, this is Joy, how can I help you?"

"Excuse me, Drake and Benton, you said?"

"Yes, Ma'am, can I help you?"

"Rick Benton, please," Abby said, slightly puzzled.

A moment later, her uncle answered, "This is Rick." His voice was confident, steady, strong as always.

"Hey, it's me. Just returning your call."

"Abby, glad you called back. You caught me at a good time. How are things?"

"All right, there's not much going on. And you?" She asked politely.

"Swell, everything's great. Hey listen, do you have some time on your hands? Could you swing by the old office?"

"Well, Steven is coming home tonight, and I thought I'd . . ."

"What time is he due?"

"Quarter to seven."

"This won't take more than an hour. I think you'll be interested."

"What's going on?"

"Oh! Listen, Abby, there's another call coming through. Well, if you make up your mind, you know where to find me."

"Well, I . . ." but he had already hung up.

Sighing once again, she glanced at her cell phone. It was only half past three. She supposed that stopping by the office wouldn't take too long. He had wanted to see her, and it had been a long time since he had even called to say hello.

Putting the keys back in the ignition, she shifted to reverse and backed out of the AMG lot. The office was only ten minutes away, and she soon found herself staring at the small building.

What caught her eye was a maintenance worker who was painting a fresh coat over the establishment's name. There it was once again: the name Benton juxtaposed with Drake.

Curious, she proceeded to open the door and found herself facing a young girl, not any older than herself. She had long, jet-black hair and wore far too much make up, in Abby's estimation.

Trying not to grimace, Abby realized this must be "Joy," her replacement. She forced a smile and asked for her uncle.

"He's in a conference right now," she said guardedly. "Can I help you with something?"

"He's expecting me," Abby said. "I'm his niece."

"In that case, follow me."

Joy led her down the familiar hallway, but to Abby's surprise, escorted her into one of the full office suites, impressively adorned with mahogany desk, bookcase, and imitation fireplace.

"I'll let him know you're here," she said and left the door open. Abby glanced around her.

She fingered a picture of her late Aunt Jane on the fireplace mantle, her mind taking in her uncle's new office. So this was why he wanted to see her. He had received a promotion and wanted her congratulations. Well, she would be polite and modest in her praise. The last thing her uncle needed was a larger ego.

"Ah, Abby, there you are. I knew you'd come."

She turned to face him standing in the doorway. Other than hints of gray in his otherwise black hair, he looked ageless. His six-foot stature, broad-shouldered build, and well-defined features had always placed him a cut above the rest. He always tried to get his way, and he usually succeeded.

"Well, I happened to be in the area."

"Have a seat, will you? Drake will be here in a moment."

"I'm really happy for you, Uncle."

"What? Oh, that! Yes, Drake officially introduced me as his partner yesterday, but well, I've kind of grown into the role over the past months.

"Sit down, sit down, I think you'll be interested in this."

"What do you mean?"

"Or maybe I should have Drake tell you himself."

"Tell me what?"

"About our proposition. Ah, here he is. Drake, you remember Abby, my niece?"

"It's a pleasure to see you again. As I recall, you were a good hand around here last summer."

Reagan Drake was probably approaching sixty but looked years younger, thanks to his excellent physical condition and mental sharpness. He was of average stature, with the looks of a bulldog, but the diplomacy of a southern gentleman.

"Good hand?" Rick echoed. "And then you jilted her like you did by bringing in your niece! Now that's some girl."

"Now, Benton, she is my niece."

"Flirts with the boys every chance she gets," Rick winked at Abby.

Drake cleared his throat and changed the subject. "Now this may seem like an unusual request, but before we say anything further, would you tell us exactly how you remember it."

"I don't understand," Abby said. "Remember what?"

"My dear, I'm sorry, but I thought Rick had told you," Drake said kindly. "We are interested in hearing your story of the events of and preceding your attack. We have reason to suspect that the affair has been conveniently 'covered up' to conceal a much larger problem.

"So you see, we'd like to hear your first-hand story. There are already enough versions floating around, thanks to the press and general gossip."

"I see," Abby said. She really didn't but trusted Drake's professionalism and her uncle's judgment.

She had tried to put the events out of her mind and paused before recounting her story.

There was a moment of silence after she finished.

"The package was never mentioned by the press," Rick murmured.

"Yes, it was only in the police statement," Drake said. "That's where I read about it, but I wanted to hear it from her mouth."

"They couldn't find it at the scene," Abby said. "So the case manager told me it was probably a hallucination of concussive disorientation or something like that. I insisted I hadn't made it up, but the subject was delicately dropped and never brought up again."

"Who's the case manager?" Drake asked.

"Jamison," Rick replied. "He seems legit, but we're doing some more background inquiries on him."

"There were no samples, no dogs used at the scene?"

"They did a clean sweep. Not a trace of PS59."

"Excuse me, of what?" Abby asked.

"PS59 is short for a new psycho-stimulant on the black market – or rumored to soon be for sale on the black market," Rick explained. "We haven't been able to get our hands on it, and every time it moves around, we miss it."

"Why's it so important?" Abby asked.

"I think we'd better start from the beginning," Drake said. "But first, as you already know, any information discussed here is absolutely confidential."

"Of course."

"Kind of like the Dawson matter last summer," Rick said. "Only that was kid's play compared to this."

Drake leaned back into his seat and began, "Where do I start? There's so much speculation surrounding the whole affair and not enough solid proof. Let me start with what little we know for sure.

"We know that within the last six months, the black market has been abuzz with rumors of a new super drug that would enhance human performance.

"We know the 'rumors' of this drug's existence are being propagated by a well-known North American terrorist organization. That's the Drug Enforcement Agency's angle anyway.

"We know that in the last month or so, that organization made an attempt to complete its first sales transaction of PS59 in Miami. The attempt went awry for all parties involved – the DEA's undercover agents included – and since then, none of the underground agents involved have been able to learn anything more.

"Now on to the speculative," Drake said. "You don't need me to tell you that many men – and women – in this world are driven by the quest for power. Just open your high school history book. How have they all sought power? By people and possessions that would enhance their position: an alliance, a new weapon, a new strategy, etc.

"But now, enters an opportunity, not to manipulate something or someone else, but to manipulate their very manpower, themselves, in short.

"This psycho-stimulant is not unlike cocaine or amphetamines in that it enhances alertfulness, memory and mood – even if the subject is sleep-deprived. Unlike those common street drugs, it does so without causing a rebound, crash or 'high.' The rumor is that this drug artificially enhances the brain and the body with seemingly no side affects."

"The human being is in many respects 'the weakest link' in warfare," Rick pointed out. "After all, a tank doesn't need sleep or rely on his alertness to discern friend or foe."

"This is all very interesting," Abby said, "but I don't understand how this relates to me – or even to Drake and Benton, since all I've heard so far is DEA involvement."

"Up to a month ago, there was only DEA involvement," Benton said. "Up to a month ago, the DEA had a definite advantage: their suspects thought themselves above suspicion.

"But that all changed after Miami. The agents realized at that point that a large-scale operation was going on and tried to nab the crooks then and there. They just didn't know how large it was – too large to take on the spur of the moment. They managed to take one of the masterminds down with them, but even that was a failure. They had secured him for questioning and then out of no where – he's shot in the back."

"Knew too much," Drake said.

"So the DEA blew their cover big time and for the last month have failed to uncover so much as a rumor, a whisper about PS59 – or who's trying to sell or buy it and why, for that matter."

"Which leads us to an interesting side note," Drake said. "The day before the Miami debacle, a young woman was clubbed in a cemetery for no apparent reason, other than a rumored package of some unidentified substance.

"And between the case officer and the press, the whole episode has been overlooked, neglected, practically forgotten, leaving the victim with little to no recourse."

"So that's me," Abby said. "So what?"

"The so what of it all is that we think the two are connected," Rick said.

"You think the package was a sample of PS59?"

"Actually, we do."

"That seems a little far-fetched. Neil had a flawless alibi, and as much as I didn't like him, it wasn't grounds to press my personal prejudices."

"Sounds like your case officer Jamison speaking," Drake said dryly.

Rick explained, "What your case officer failed to mention was that Neil has a rather shady history."

"He's been involved with crime?"

"Oh, his high school records show misdemeanors like petty theft, bullying in high school, carjacking and things of that nature," Benton said.

"I could have told you that," Abby said.

"But don't you find it strange that someone with so many problems in high school seemingly dropped off the map the last seven years?"

"He would tell you he had mended his ways," Abby rolled her eyes.

"Yes, I'm sure he would," Drake said. "But your uncle here has been doing his homework. DeWitt's high school record is enough material for any officer to want to keep an eye on him. But no one has, because he's off the radar."

"I don't understand."

"Abby, our suspicion is that Neil moved from gang-related crimes to organized crime; that if we can uncover the man he has become, we'll find evidence to point to the mastermind behind him."

There was a definite pause in the conversation. Abby's mind whirled as she allowed her old suspicions to surface. Had her intuition been right? But what did it matter?

"How does this involve me?"

Benton glanced at Drake, who nodded back. "Abby," Rick began, "What would you say to coming back on staff here as my personal assistant. You'd be filing my reports, writing briefs, same kinds of things you did last year.

"But one thing would be different. If I traveled on assignment, you'd come with me. You would be a personal secretary instead of the office receptionist."

"I'm flattered, but I hate to think you're hiring me just because of your interest in a case," Abby said.

"It's not just that," Drake said. "You're a hard worker, you're already in the system, and we could add you to the payroll tomorrow."

"But it is the case at the same time," Benton said. "Think of it this way, Abby. You're our only real witness. Even though you didn't see who attacked you, you used your instinct. My guts tell me you're on to something. Even if it wasn't DeWitt who clubbed you over the head, whoever it was must have been after that package."

"So what will I have to do?"

"We just described your job description, no strings attached. We're not asking you to do any investigating – au contraire. You're just a witness in this case."

"We would like to schedule a time to go over everything from the very beginning – when you met DeWitt, your reservations about him, and things he said," Rick said.

"We were just hoping we could have that conversation while you're on the clock," Drake smiled. "I'm sorry if we seemed to have slighted you earlier this summer, but we would like to have you back."

"Well, I am interested," Abby said.

"Wonderful," Rick said. "I know your brother's arriving in town tonight. How about you give me a call sometime tomorrow? You have my cell number."

"Of course. I appreciate the offer," Abby said, rising. She shook hands with both men, managed some polite small talk and then left.

Drake and Benton watched her walk down the hallway.

"She's a good kid," Drake said. "I hate to see her mixed up in this business."

"I'd hate to see her get hurt again," Benton said. "Not only is she my niece, but like I said, she's our only witness.

"And sooner or later, DeWitt and whomever he's in league with are going to wise up to that fact. I'd prefer she's working for us at the time, instead of working drive through at McDonalds."

Chapter 8

New Developments

✢

Abby glanced over her glass of tea at her twin brother. He had changed. He was surer of himself and practically bursting with stories.

He would be home two weeks, and she would make the most of them. She still hadn't told anyone but her parents about her job offer, which she had already decided to take. It would be the same routine office work, but it would make her feel independent, at least of the mission. Maybe someday, she would have her own stories to tell.

She caught Andrew staring at her several times during the evening, but she tried to avoid him. Sometimes, she felt he could see right through her.

"Do you mind if I stop by during the week?" Steven was asking Jimmy. "I'd like to help out with the planes where I can."

"Of course," Jimmy replied. "Wait till you see what Andrew's done with old *Wings*," and he took up the story.

Abby listened, remembering her brother and Andrew playing in the DC-3 as children. Both had once dreamed of being pilots until Stephen took up an avid interest in history and archeology, and Andrew's poor vision made him settle for airplane mechanics.

She too had been fascinated with flight, but less with the actual act of flying and more with the concept of where planes could take you.

"Maybe you can give Abby and Kim a hand with the mailings, if you find us too boring," Matt joked.

"What do you say to that, Sis?" Stephen grinned.

"Uh, well, it would be fun, but really, I don't know," Abby fumbled with her words, caught off guard by the question. She had intended to tell her brothers of her job offer, but not tonight.

Mrs. Grant came to her rescue. "Abby's been offered a job by your Uncle Rick to work in the office again."

"He finally came around?" Stephen asked. "Didn't he offer the job to someone else?"

"It's a different job, but a paying one," Abby insisted. "And I'm going to take it."

Everyone seemed happy for her, and the conversation turned to other things, specifically, a get-together Matt and Jimmy wanted to plan for that coming Friday, only two days away.

But as Abby followed Steven to the front porch to wish Matt and Jimmy a good night, Andrew gently pulled her aside while the others went ahead.

"What's the matter?" Abby asked, swatting at a mosquito. The sun had since slipped beneath the horizon, and the porch lamp was attracting all manner of flying insects.

"Abby, I can't put my finger on it, that's just it," he said, removing his glasses to wipe away a smudge. "It's just that I know you're eager for this summer job, and I'm happy you've finally got a paying job, but why all of a sudden?"

"What do you mean?"

"I mean, why did they wait so long to offer you a job if they liked you so much? You proved yourself last summer, and what a headache you had of things! So why now?"

"I'm just glad for a job, that's all," Abby tried to shy away.

"It's about that funny business in St. Vincent, isn't it? Is that why they're suddenly interested?"

"Maybe, I don't care. It's a good job, and I'm going to take it. I'm bored, tired of just sitting around and doing nothing."

"So working at the mission is your definition of 'doing nothing'?" Andrew asked slowly.

"It's just so slow, and I don't feel I'm really making a difference, licking stamps and typing letters and sorting mail."

"Abby, those letters mean a great deal. They share the hearts of the missionaries, share prayer requests, and keep the supporters up to date on how they can be praying for the ministry.

"If you don't think office work makes a difference, what do you think about my work – servicing planes, working mechanics? When it's slow, I'm just a general maintenance worker, keeping things running smoothly so the pilots can fly on schedule and so the shipments arrive on time.

"So what you're saying is that only the pilots really get a chance to serve God, that all our 'minor' tasks are meaningless."

"That's not what I'm saying at all," Abby snapped. "And what does this conversation have to do with my accepting Rick's offer? I'm just saying that I'd rather do something important, not just sit around. I suppose I'd rather be a pilot – to stick to your analogy."

As soon as the words left her mouth, Abby wished she hadn't said them. But it was too late.

"So would I, Abby," Andrew said slowly, stepping aside, and placing his glasses back on his nose. "But then, I've learned God works behind the scenes too. He prefers faithfulness to front seat driving."

Abby winced as she watched her friend walk away. She saw him climb into Matt's car as Steven waved goodbye to Jimmy.

The front porch lamp distorted her perspective, casting shadows, making the fading car lights seem to flicker before they actually disappeared out of sight.

She winced again at Andrew's words, which struck an unsettling cord inside her. Maybe it was she who was seeing through smudged lenses, not Andrew, after all.

— — — — — — — — — — — — — —

The next morning, Abby pulled up in front of Drake and Benton, parked her car, and stepped onto the pavement.

Rick had been delighted when she phoned him, accepting the position. He had asked her to stop by to take care of some paperwork.

He told her that her first full day would be tomorrow, which was Friday. His real reason for wanting her to come into the office today was to review a "busy agenda" he was preparing.

Abby had wanted to know if it involved her as well, but another call had come in, and their connection had ended.

Joy hustled her off to her uncle's office with a terse, "This way please," and left her in the empty room.

Abby could hardly believe it had been only yesterday when she had sat there and retold her story to Drake and Rick.

It all seemed so surreal. She remembered her conversation with Andrew and tried to shake off a feeling of uneasiness.

Abby tried to sort it out. Sure, Andrew was concerned about her. He had always acted like a third brother. She had given up reminding him that she already had two brothers, because he never listened.

And yet, though he cared about her welfare, she had sensed he was worried about something more than that. After all, he was happy she would be able to have a steady income for the summer.

It was something else, something that seemed harder for her to face.

"Ah, there you are, Abby," Rick's booming voice interrupted her thoughts.

"Uncle," she smiled, trying to sound more confident than she felt.

"Just a couple of formalities, you know," he said, handing her a clipboard. Abby recognized the terms of employment forms.

"I'll be back in a minute," he said.

Abby glanced at her pen with a sigh and began filling out the general paperwork. A few minutes later, her uncle reappeared, noticeably impatient.

"Done with those forms yet?"

"Yes, quite," Abby said, handing them back.

"There's so much we need to go over with you, and the day already seems wasted," he said, escorting her to the conference room.

"More paperwork, I suppose," Abby tried to laugh lightly.

"Oh that," Rick said absently. "We already took care of that last night."

"But I thought . . ."

"I figured you wouldn't refuse," he said with a disarming smile. "Nope, we've already run you through the hoops, as it were."

Abby furrowed her brow but thought best not to argue. She had seen Rick in this mood several times before and knew better than to interrupt when he was determined to have his way.

Without knocking, he opened the conference door and stepped aside for Abby to enter.

She blinked in surprise. Assembled around the table were Drake and two other people. The first was a blonde middle-aged woman in a suit, fingering through two folders to her right. The other was a man in his late twenties or early thirties, dressed in casual attire but with a serious expression that changed to a smile when she entered.

Rick indicated a seat next to Drake, and Abby gratefully slid into it after shaking hands and general introductions.

The lady was Ms. Edith Brightly, administrative assistant to the gentleman, Agent Garth Owens.

Ms. Brightly smiled reservedly at Abby, who managed to smile awkwardly back. Though not unkind, her eyes seemed to sum her up, and Abby sensed that for some reason, she disapproved.

Drake immediately took charge of the conversation. "Well, now that we've all met, let's get started. Edith, why don't you explain all the paperwork first? You're a busy woman, and there's no need for you to sit through the entire briefing."

She nodded and passed two folders to Rick. "Those are your travel documents, including passports. I've contacted Agent Ward, who will be your key liaison in Nassau. As previously discussed, he will meet you at the airport.

"You'll find other travel information, as well as primary contact information. Your assistant will need to understand the daily reporting procedures. I'll address those with her once you're finished here.

"Other than that, everything is quite self-explanatory – even complete with maps and tourist guides," she said with a wry smile.

"Thank you, Edith, that will be all for now," Garth said.

"Very good. Let me know if you require anything more," she said, rising.

"We'll make sure you and Miss Grant have some time together this afternoon."

Miss Grant. Abby suddenly realized he was talking about her – Edith had been talking about her.

"I'm sorry, I don't understand," Abby looked at her uncle who was busy reviewing the folders.

"This one's yours," he said, handing it to her.

"Mine?"

Rick only smiled at her.

"I apologize for your confusion, Miss Grant, but it's always good to get the preliminaries out of the way first," Drake explained.

"I apologize as well," Owens said and melted away her worries with a warm smile. Abby immediately thought of Dixie and what her response would be to this agent's winsome ways. He had dark brown eyes, jet-black hair, and a muscular build. "I was under the impression you had already received a general briefing. I'm sorry if some of this material seems new to you."

"Some of it?" Abby found her voice. "I have no idea what's going on here."

"Partly my fault," Rick admitted. "I didn't have time to chat. I just made sure that Joy had taken care of her end of the paperwork."

"Where did you leave off?" Owens asked Abby.

"I'm just getting started," she faltered. "Yesterday, my uncle – Mr. Benton – and Mr. Drake offered me a position as Rick's assistant. They told me I would be filing briefs and doing paperwork – things I did last summer as an intern."

"They did express their interest in a certain case involving yourself, I understand?"

"Well, yes, but they expressed a desire to discuss it after I had resumed working here. I hadn't sensed an urgency about the matter, only an interest."

"There's been a twist since yesterday," Rick interrupted. "Interest has turned to urgency, and that's why Garth flew from DC last night to meet us."

"Washington DC?" Abby asked.

"I work for the DEA," Garth explained.

"Of course," Abby replied, her tone nothing short of incredulous.

"Let's start at the beginning," Drake said, sensing the teenager's agitation.

"The very beginning," Owens agreed, and again, Abby couldn't help but think that he personified Hollywood's handsome agent. Rugged square jaw, handsome eyes, broad smile . . .

"Let's pick up where we left off yesterday," Rick interrupted, and Abby ruefully thought to herself that he personified the ugly reality.

"We told you about the sting in Miami that went south."

"That was my sting," Owens admitted. "We thought we were dealing with small scale black market smugglers. We couldn't have been more wrong.

"Since then, I've done my homework on some of the more predominant organizations at work, or that we now suspect may be at work behind the scenes. One that's been on the corner of the radar for decades but really hasn't surfaced much in North America is El GATO."

"El GATO?" Abby asked skeptically. "Look, I took Spanish in high school. What's so fearsome about an organization called 'the cat'?"

"That's what we've thought for years, perhaps foolishly so," Owens said. "Your uncle has actually had a couple run-ins with this group in the past."

"We're not exactly the best of friends," Rick muttered, "but that's another story for another day. Look, don't let the name El GATO fool you. This group is headed by a former KGB agent named Vladimir Zarchoff and is actually an acronym that stands for The Greater American Terrorist Organization."

"Terrorist organization?" Abby found her voice again. "I thought we were talking about drug smuggling?"

"Again, that's what the DEA thought about this activity in Miami," Owens said. "But now, we think we may have just scratched the surface of something bigger than some small sales going on in the black market."

"Which had been oddly silent about the whereabouts of PS59 – until last night," Drake added. "The DEA received an anonymous tip about a sale going down somewhere in the Bahamas. A sale of PS59."

"What you all just said about Miami made me think of something," Abby said.

"Yes?" Owens asked.

"When I asked Neil – that is, DeWitt – what he did for a living, he said that he was an inside sales rep for a manufacturing firm located out of Miami. I suppose that may not mean anything . . ."

"But it just might. What did he say he manufactured?"

"He said he didn't manufacture anything and made some condescending remark about having to explain the role of an inside sales rep," Abby wrinkled her nose at the memory.

"I wonder if he were telling the truth, in a roundabout way," Rick said. "Perhaps his organization doesn't sell direct."

"Or, he was indicating that his role in the organization is strictly marketing," Drake mused.

"But anyway, I suppose if he's above suspicion, that's irrelevant," Abby said.

"We suspect him for the very reason that he seems above suspicion," Rick checked her, "and no, it's not irrelevant. That's partly why we wanted you on board. You may remember things – a phrase, a comment, a clue – as we go along.

"But let's get back to the issue at hand. The tip indicated the sale would go down by June 17th. That's next Wednesday, a week from yesterday."

"Agent Ward and another colleague have been following the lead from Nassau, and we want a small team to join them undercover, as it were," Owens explained.

"That's where we come in," Rick said.

"We?" Abby asked.

"Open up your file."

Abby found herself staring at her own picture on a passport she had never applied for.

"I don't understand how this involves me. I just started my summer job – 15 minutes ago."

"It involves your so-called accident three weeks ago," Owens said. "That was the day before we messed up Miami, and we're becoming more certain the two are connected.

"We've been keeping an eye on DeWitt since then. Sure, he seems all above board, but his inside sales job has coincidentally taken him to the Bahamas.

"And you and he have a history together. Besides, you're the only person who has actually come into contact with Starch," Owens said.

"Starch?" Abby asked.

"That's a nickname for PS59, or so we've learned recently," Rick explained. "It makes sense, in a roundabout way. It's a psycho-stimulant that provides a prolonged source of high-intensity energy. On a larger scale, it works like the way carbohydrates provide your body with fuel."

"So you're sure that's what I found under the porch and at the cemetery?" Abby asked.

"As sure as we can be without having proof," Owens chuckled.

"Which is also where you come into play," Drake began slowly. "You're our only witness who can identify the substance. Surely it had some distinguishing factor."

"Smell," Abby replied. "Sickly sweet."

"At any event, we've hired you as my personal assistant," Rick said, "so if you prefer, you may consider your relationship with the case strictly professional."

"Meaning?"

"Whither I go, you will go, and I'm going to Nassau."

Abby looked down at her folder. She knew Rick made references to the Bible only pragmatically. He never really thought about the context.

And what would her mother say? But she guessed her mom didn't really have a say. She had signed those employment papers, and if she wanted to keep her job, she had to go.

It would be adventuresome. The thought of traveling out of the country, investigating criminal activity sounded like something out of a Nancy Drew novel she'd read as a middle school student.

It was her uncle that bothered her the most – his conceit, his assumption that she would just fall in line according to his plan. After all, this passport staring her in the face was made long before she had walked into the office that morning. She could just say no thank you and walk out.

Or, she could embrace it.

"When are we leaving?" she asked and met her uncle's eyes with a steady smile.

Chapter 9

Engine Trouble

I t was only seven o'clock in the morning, and already Andrew was on his second cup of coffee. Ian was on his third.

The Cessna would be laid up for weeks, depending on when they could get the parts and when they would have enough time to overhaul the engine. Andrew would have his work cut out for him, and everyone would have to chip in.

They would need time. And where would they get the money? They were on budget, but there was not enough right at the moment to finance an engine overhaul.

Andrew looked up as his brother walked into the hangar. He hadn't wanted to ask him to come in on his day off, but he had to.

"Hey, Brother, thanks for coming."

"I couldn't sleep anyway," Matt managed a wry smile. He turned to Ian who summed up the situation. He was already working on an estimate. When he finished, he nearly took Matt's breath away.

"There's no way we're going to make both the Port-au-Prince and the Nassau flights," Matt said, shoulders sagging, "especially since the N700 is overdue for routine maintenance."

"It's not impossible," Andrew disagreed.

"That leaves us with only one DC-3," Ian pointed out.

"Two," Andrew corrected.

Both men just stared at their mechanic.

"I said two, and I mean two," Andrew said. "You're forgetting *Wings.*"

Matt's face spoke volumes of his doubt. The plane was too old. Its flying days were over. It hadn't flown since they were boys.

"I said *Wings,* and I mean *Wings,*" Andrew insisted. "After all, do you think I spend my evenings and weekends pouring my time and energy into a model plane? No Sirs, she's going to fly again, and she's practically ready.

"I'm confident she could make the short flight to Nassau with no trouble. Besides, it's just a cargo run, unlike the Port-au-Prince passenger flight."

Andrew made his case. Instead of worrying about the estimate for the engine, Ian pulled out a clean sheet of paper and started making his notes. Matt and Andrew waited quietly. They had worked around the veteran pilot and assistant manager long enough to know that he thought on paper.

"If she's as ready as you say she is, I think we could add enough checks and balances to the flight schedule to take into account any plane trouble you might encounter," he said at last.

"Instead of a day turnaround, we could keep her grounded long enough for Andrew to do a thorough inspection. I can look into renting a hangar for a night.

"Of course, Andrew, that means you'd have to go along."

He pretended to be disappointed. "Ah well, there goes my time off. At least I'm current on my passport!"

"Jimmy's scheduled as my co-pilot," Matt said, turning to Ian. "Both of us are familiar with the old DC-3."

"Well, that's that," Ian said, scribbling a final note to himself. "Andrew, it's time you make good on your promise that she's flight-worthy before I start making the phone calls."

"With pleasure."

"You know that if this doesn't work, I'm going to have to call our people in Nassau and cancel," Ian said.

"She'll fly again, Captain," Andrew grinned. "*Wings* was a God-send when we first got her. She was old then; she's older now.

"But who said you have to be in mint condition for God to use you? If that were the case, we'd all be parked on the sidelines."

Ian had to laugh. "All right, Andrew, come along before you start a sermon."

The three men started walking to the edge of the property where the craft was parked. No one said a word. Ian was thinking about the pre-flight work and paperwork involved in getting the plane back on the active list. Matt was hoping that his brother wasn't as sleep-deprived as he looked.

Andrew was envisioning *Wings* rising to face the horizon and a new day.

———————————————

"What did you say?" Jimmy asked, practically dropping his cell phone. Steven took his eyes off the road for just a minute to look at his brother, whose jaw seemed nearly unhinged.

"I can't believe it. And she passed Ian's pre-flight inspection? Flying colors? Incredible. You're not just pulling my leg, are you?

"All right, all right, I'm hearing you loud and clear. We'll be there in five minutes," Jimmy said. He flipped his phone shut and whistled.

"What's going on?" Steven asked.

"Matt just told me that Ian's approved *Wings of the Dawn* to fly to the Bahamas this coming Monday afternoon. I can barely believe it."

"So Andrew did it after all. He told me he was going to work on her when I left after graduation, but I didn't think he meant to make her fly again."

They pulled into the parking lot and jumped out. Andrew and Matt met them half way.

For a moment, they were boys again. Gone were the cares of financial responsibility, house payments, career moves. They were middle-schoolers, shooting off rockets in their backyard, lighting fireworks just to see how far they could fly.

Wings had captured their boyhood fascination. They wanted to fly. They wanted to go places. They wanted to discover new things.

Ian's voice from inside the hangar interrupted them, and the four raced inside.

"There you are," he said. "I just got clearance from Nassau.

"And do I have news for you. When I told my friend Lawrence about you all needing a place to spend the night, he said he would take care of it and rambled on about how excited his church would be to have you. Turns out, they're having a ground-breaking ceremony for a new building. Apparently, they lost their old building to a fire, and it's taken them longer than they had hoped to start the new construction project."

"When's the ceremony?" Jimmy asked.

"It's actually Tuesday morning, and I had initially planned for you to fly back that day."

"You want us to stay just for a ceremony?" Matt raised an eyebrow.

Ian laughed. "The groundbreaking ceremony is in the morning, but the 'real work' is going to begin that afternoon. They're just getting started on the building. They could use some extra manpower, I gather.

"I told him I'd give him a call back. I don't know if you fellows can squeeze two to three extra days into your schedules or not. We always like to help our missionaries where we can, and well, this opportunity seems to fall into place."

"I think that would be great," Jimmy said, "as long as you can spare all three of us."

"The rest of next week is pretty quiet, as far as the schedule goes," Ian said.

"Works fine with me," Andrew said.

"Any chance you could use an extra hand?" Steven piped up. "I'm home for the next few weeks and had planned to help out the guys here. My passport's current, and I don't mind getting dirty."

"Sounds like we might have a plan," Ian smiled.

———————————————

Abby stepped onto the front porch, reached for the door and paused. She could hear several voices all talking at once and was surprised, and slightly annoyed, to find that her family had company.

The door swung open, and Steven nearly collided into her with a bear hug.

"What's going on?" she asked.

"You'll never believe it," he said, playfully pushing her into the living room where Matt, Jimmy and Andrew were gathered.

"Believe what?" Abby asked. "Did I miss someone's birthday?"

"This is better than a birthday," Steven said. "We're going to the Bahamas on *Wings of the Dawn!*"

"*Wings of the Dawn?*" Abby asked. "But I thought she'd never fly again?"

"Nothing's impossible," Andrew grinned.

"Isn't that the truth," Abby muttered.

"Ian actually offered for you to come along since he knew how much you wanted to spend time with your brother," Andrew said. "But then we had to tell him you'd found a different job."

"Kim and Amber are pleading to go in your stead," Matt said. "They've got plans to make the flight a full-fledge mission trip."

"They would," Steven laughed.

Abby managed a low chuckle and disappeared into her room. Andrew shot Steven a questioning glance, but his friend merely shrugged.

She reappeared in the hallway a moment later, pulled open the hall closet, and started yanking at something in the back.

"Sis?" Steven asked.

Abby turned and smiled mischievously back at him. "Oh, don't mind me, but I've got my own trip to pack for."

A pile of small boxes tumbled out of the closet along with the suitcase and scattered across the floor. Her own story came out much along the same lines – rambled, slightly incoherent, and nearly unbelievable, even to her own ears.

That was yesterday. When she woke up the next morning to see her bag packed, her passport in her purse, and her friends' best wishes still ringing in her ears, she knew it was no dream.

She tried to ignore the knot in her stomach by reminding herself of the same assurances she had told her parents.

She was just a personal secretary. She would just be filing the reports – yes, those dreadful reports that Ms. Brightly had drilled into her memory. She would just be a cover, an assistant under the guise of a tourist.

She would be playing the part of a niece on vacation with her rich uncle. He was after all her uncle, so how hard could her part be?

She would only be gone a week at the most. She would be back before the AMG team returned and probably resume a boring job for the rest of the summer.

Those words now seemed empty to her. She felt a strange tingling sensation, a mixture of excitement and nerves.

She had kissed her family goodbye that morning and now waited for her uncle to pick her up. It was a quarter to ten. He should be here any minute.

Dixie had called her last night and pulled most of the story out of her – minus the confidential details. She had practically swooned at the thought of going to the Bahamas. She had no idea the trip might involve her renegade cousin.

Abby peeked out the blinds just in time to see a silver sedan pull into the circular drive. Taking a deep breath and pulling her suitcase behind her, she opened the front door to greet her uncle who looked smooth and collected in a Hawaiian shirt and cargo shorts.

"Are you ready, Niece?"

"As ever, Uncle," Abby smiled.

"You look the part," he smiled approvingly at her plaid Bermuda shorts and tank top. He whisked her luggage into the trunk as she opened the passenger door.

"What's this?"

"Oh that," Rick said. "It's just a little something for the trip."

"It's mine?" Abby just stared at the camera.

"It was actually Owens' idea," Rick grinned. "He seemed quite impressed with you."

"My own digital camera?" Abby asked.

Rick laughed as he started the engine. "Well, he wanted you to look authentic as a tourist, so there you go. Don't just stand there looking at it. We've got a plane to catch."

Abby spent the ride to the airport testing her camera, making breathless remarks about its features, and trying to figure out how some of the more advanced modes worked.

Rick spent most of the ride laughing at her and telling her to read the manual.

As they were checking in their luggage, Rick's phone rang.

"Rick here," he said, handing the attendant his bag. He frowned slightly and then hung up.

"Is everything okay, Uncle?" Abby asked.

"Wrong number, that's all," he smiled tersely.

Half an hour later, they had boarded the plane and were squeezing through the aisle to their seats. A short, stocky man stared up at Abby from his seat before engrossing himself in a newspaper.

Abby glanced back at him, and in doing so, almost tripped over a stout woman who had stopped dead in the aisle to bicker with another man about her seat.

"Pay attention, Abby, and stop staring at people," Rick muttered under his breath.

Abby slid into her own seat by the window and whispered back, "I'm not staring at people."

"What about the guy with the newspaper?"

"He stared at me first."

Rick rolled his eyes. "Just relax, okay? We're not even there yet."

She could imagine how Edith Brightly would sum up the situation. Notebook in hand, she would place a check mark next to Abby's name and write, "Scolded for staring at stranger."

Abby involuntarily shuddered. That woman was far too cold and serious for her taste. She would probably tear apart her daily reports.

But Abby refused to think about Edith Brightly today. She was going to the colorful Bahamas, and nothing, short of an encounter with Neil himself, could steal her joy.

In what seemed to her no time at all, Abby and Rick had disembarked at the Nassau airport, breezed through customs, and stood waiting in the terminal.

"What does he look like?" Abby asked.

"You mean Ward?" Rick chuckled. "Look for a tall, Bahamian native."

"Tall Bahamian man," Abby repeated to herself.

A deep voice behind her made her jump.

"You must be Miss Abigail."

She whirled around to face the tallest Bahamian man she had ever seen. He must have been at least six-feet, six-inches tall, and his muscular build made him appear even taller.

Everything about him was broad – broad shoulders, broad chest, broad smile – very broad smile.

"Good to see you again, Benton," he said, shaking Rick's hand. Abby winced when he reached for hers, and he laughed a deep, booming laugh.

Rick winked. "He's a gentle giant."

"Only when the ladies are around," he corrected with a grin, escorting them to the luggage claim. Rick grabbed his bag, and Coby whisked Abby's off the belt as if it were one of the toy pieces of wooden furniture she had played with as a girl.

He flung the luggage into the back of his red pick-up truck, and Abby found herself squeezed between the two men.

With the windows cranked low, Coby sped away, driving on the left side of the road, weaving through a mess of traffic with remarkable agility.

Though his front windshield was muddy and slightly cracked, it afforded Abby her first real look at the Bahamas from the ground.

They passed colorful, yet often faded buildings. The roads were narrow and busy with poor or non-existent sidewalks. The vegetation was lush but rarely trimmed or kept.

"It seems rather earthy, run down or just run wild," Abby remarked with disappointment.

Coby chuckled. "Earthy is a good way to put it. But the Bahamas has her beautiful side as well. Wait till you see the beaches, Bay Street, and her historical side. If you want to describe the Bahamas, describe her as alive.

"People here live life and tell life the way they know it – with no frills or reservations," Coby continued.

"Not rated," Rick winked at Abby, who shot him a reproachful glance.

"But don't go comparing the Bahamas to your home," Coby said. "The culture here is totally different. The people don't run on Eastern time. They run on Bahama time."

Abby resumed staring out the window, trying to distract herself from the stuffy, sticky inside of the truck's cab.

Coby interrupted her thoughts again. "So tell me about yourself, Miss Abigail. When Benton told me he was bringing his niece for the trip, my mother could barely contain herself. I think she'll be disappointed to find you're not quite the wisp of a girl she imagined. I'll have to tell the fellows to go easy on you."

Abby blushed and hurriedly interrupted, "Please, just call me Abby. Most people do. And really, there's not too much to tell. It's rather a long story how I managed to be here, and I'm sure Rick would do a better job telling it.

"But tell me about yourself. What is it you do here?"

Coby laughed hard. "Officially, I'm a fisherman. Unofficially, well . . ."

"We've known each other a long time," Rick said.

"And we sure do have some stories," Coby agreed. "But I'll tell you a little about myself, if you want to know."

The minutes flew by as Coby began talking. Abby decided that he could have been a master storyteller with his romantic Bahamian accent and flair for telling things the way they were.

He talked about his fishing boats and how he had acquired them. He explained that his father had been a fisherman and that he had learned the trade from him. When his father was unable to manage the business, he and some of his brothers had taken over.

"Still, one of my brothers went into the tourism business," he said. "Don't be surprised. Practically three in every four jobs are in the tourism business. Even my mom sells straw products at the Straw Market. We call her our Straw Lady.

"Well, here we are," Coby said, pulling into his driveway. Abby placed both feet onto the ground and welcomed the fresh, though humid air. The truck's cab had nearly been unbearable with all three crammed inside.

Abby assumed that Coby did very well with his business, official or otherwise. A private drive led to the house which was not visible from the road. The building itself was two stories with a disconnected garage to the left. Blooming flowers, lanky trees, and well-kept green shrubbery adorned the lawn.

A light breeze played through the trees, bringing with it a faint salty scent. Abby guessed the beach couldn't be too far beyond the trees in the backyard. Stiff from the plane ride and truck cab's close quarters, she found herself wishing for a swim.

Coby must have guessed her thoughts. "As soon as we get you two settled in, why doesn't Abby take some time exploring the beach?"

"I'd love to, if that's okay with you, Rick," she said.

"Take the early afternoon off," he said generously. "We'll get to work around 3 p.m. Besides, Coby and I have some matters to discuss privately."

He gave her a terse smile and grabbed his bag from the truck's bed. Abby's own smile faded slightly at her uncle's tone, and she was reminded again that this was no pleasure trip.

Looking longingly toward the private beach, she sighed. She would enjoy the Bahamas as much as she could, while she could.

She had a feeling the next few days would be anything but fun in the sun.

Coby led the way to the house with Rick right behind him and Abby trailing behind. She skipped up the front steps just in time to catch the screen door before it closed.

Inside, the house was quiet, and Abby assumed Coby's family was at work. She wondered how many of his brothers still lived at home, and for that matter, why someone Coby's age might still live at home.

Coby soon answered her unspoken question. He led them up the stairs to two guest rooms across the hall from each other. "Please make yourselves at home," he said, opening the door to Abby's room.

"My parent's room is downstairs, and if you need anything, let them know. My place is just down the beach, but it's more of a bachelor's joint."

"I'll join you downstairs in a minute," Rick called to Coby as Abby closed her door to freshen up and unpack.

She dropped her suitcase on the floor and nearly squealed with delight when she realized her room led to a small balcony. Sure enough, from its perch, she could see the sandy, private beach behind the estate.

Rick had given her permission to explore and knowing Rick, she didn't dare ask for permission again. She would take this one opportunity to be selfish before settling down to strictly business.

Quickly unzipping her suitcase, she slipped on her swimsuit and a pair of beach shorts, stepped into some flip-flops and helped herself out the back door. She was half way to the beach when she realized she had forgotten her camera.

She quietly re-entered the kitchen door and climbed the stairs to her room. She could hear Rick and Coby's muffled voices in the living room and did not want to disturb them.

Abby had almost reached the kitchen with her camera when she stopped short. She distinctly heard Coby say her name.

"Yes, I know it sounds crazy, but she really has no idea," Rick continued. "She thinks she's here because I need an assistant to type up reports."

"Then everything I've heard about her incident is true? You think she really was on to something?"

"Why else have we been receiving these?" Rick paused a moment. "Yes, those are what you think they are. Innocent little inquiries are being made about her location, her activity. In short, someone is keeping a close eye on her – to see if she remembers anything or knows more than she seems to."

"Does she?"

"I don't know. But that doesn't matter if someone is under the impression she does."

"Why on earth did you bring her with you then?"

"As Drake says, she's our only real witness. The DEA hasn't been able to scrape together a shred of evidence that it's El GATO and not some other group behind this business. She's handled PS59 and perhaps has even been in contact with one of the affair's masterminds. It seems more risky not to keep her close at hand."

"And she just happens to be your niece."

Rick laughed. "It's all rather complicated, but it's all rather convenient. The fact that I'm her uncle and have already crossed paths with El GATO ... Let's just say the DEA made my agency an irresistible offer to take up this case."

Abby's mind was spinning as she fumbled for the screen door's latch, blinking back hot tears. She couldn't listen anymore. She had heard too much already.

The words kept playing over in her mind. Her uncle was referring to their relationship as merely convenient. His dishonesty with her, his lack of trust, burned.

She turned sharply toward the beach, nearly colliding with someone in the way. All she could discern was a tall youth with a surprised expression on his face. Mumbling an excuse, she took off in a hard run toward the beach.

Her breath finally caught in her lungs, and she fell to the ground. Abby wasn't sure how far she had run, but running had helped her vent her frustration. With her body tired, she could now think more clearly.

She knew that she needed to act as though she hadn't overheard anything. Act as if everything were novel and fresh to her. Act like the giddy, clueless girl her uncle expected her to be, thought her to be.

Rick really didn't know her at all. Sometimes, she thought he hadn't noticed her grow up over the years and wondered if he still thought of her as a little girl. He sure treated her like one.

"Oh, God, what have I gotten myself into?" Abby thought, running her fingers through the sand. The events of the last few days – the last few hours – made her head swim. "Why do I always jump into things head first?"

She pulled her knees into her stomach and hugged herself, staring at the ocean before her. She tried to pray, but her mind kept replaying her uncle's words.

"There you are," a voice startled her. "I thought I'd have to chase you clear to Cable Beach."

It was the same youth she had nearly collided with minutes ago. Only, he wasn't quite as young as he had first appeared, and Abby guessed he might just be a few years younger than her.

"I'm Freddy, Coby's brother," he said, settling down into the sand beside her. "Are you okay?"

"I'm fine," she said, rising suddenly. She acted preoccupied with brushing the sand off her shorts.

"Are you sure?"

"Something just upset me; that's all. It's really nothing worth mentioning." With that, she looked up to smile becomingly at him. It worked. He soon forgot about her tears in an effort to show off his knowledge of the beach and point out landmarks.

He reminded her very much of Coby – seemingly carefree and very friendly.

"You must be Abigail, then," he finally realized that he hadn't asked her name. "Mom said I might have to show you around, and I wasn't too thrilled about babysitting. But, well, you're not such a baby after all."

"Sorry to disappoint."

"Oh no. I think we'll have a splendid time."

Splendid, Abby thought to herself. Well, she was supposed to act like a tourist having a wonderful time with her uncle.

She would act the part her uncle had cast her to play. But behind the mask, she resolved to show Rick Benton the character of a young woman he had never taken the time to know.

Chapter 10

The Man in the Flowered Hat

"I can't believe we're going!" Those were the words that Jimmy, Matt, Steven and Andrew had to listen to over and over again as the Marshall girls exulted over their latest success. They would be going to the Bahamas on *Wings* and be working with a church that their home church supported.

The guys could only marvel at Kim and Amber's ability to make connections. The girls remembered that during their first year of high school, a missionary couple from the Bahamas had come to their church on deputation. The missionaries had taught their Sunday school class, and the girls had watched their two young children in the nursery.

That couple, Edward and Alathea Brown, were now pastoring a church on the outskirts of Nassau. Their church had been burned to the ground, and although some suspected arson, the church family was trying to put the fire behind them and focus on building for the future.

Long story short, the girls would be staying with the Browns, while the guys lodged in some economy, yet clean hotel rooms.

They would still fly in to Nassau Monday afternoon, but instead of flying out the next day, they would stay through Wednesday and leave Thursday morning.

That was Ian Smitt's doing. Jimmy and Matt had both voiced their concerns about an extended stay and how the mission would be shorthanded, but he had waived their fears aside. With two planes down, the pilots' absence would not be a hardship.

If anyone, Andrew would be missed the most, Ian had teased. Their best mechanic away during an engine overhaul did seem problematic.

But again, Ian had solved the problem. He knew a friend who knew a friend, and to make another long story short, they would have the qualified mechanics needed for the task.

"I can't believe we're going!" Amber hummed to herself, buzzing around the hangar like a bee that had lost its flower.

"Over here," Andrew called out with a sigh, waiting for Amber to hand him the tool he had asked her to bring him.

"Sorry, but I . . ."

"I know, you can't believe you're going," he rolled his eyes and claimed his tool. Andrew was putting some finishing touches on the DC-3 while the pilots went over flight plans. Steven and Kim had since left to pick up some lunch for the group.

"So have you heard from Abby yet?" Amber asked, sitting down on one of the workbenches.

"Not yet," he said. "She just left this morning, you know."

"It doesn't take that long to get to the Bahamas."

"Well, why should I be the first to hear from her? Ask Steve."

Amber arched an eyebrow. "Now, Andrew, she always calls you. You're like best friends."

Andrew did not reply and appeared to be concentrating on his work.

"Did you guys fight?"

Andrew turned around to look at her. "What are you talking about? Why would we fight?"

"I don't know, but you got awfully quiet when I mentioned Abby. I figured something was up."

"Girls and connections," Andrew thought to himself.

"Look, if you don't want to talk, that's fine with me."

"There's nothing to talk about."

"Oh really."

Andrew dropped his tools and whirled to face her. He felt the blood rush to his face, started to say something and then thought better.

"Look, Amber, I'm sorry. You're right. I'm not being myself. Yes, Abby and I didn't part on the best terms. We had a disagreement – I guess you could call it.

"That was Wednesday. I only saw her briefly on Thursday, and now she's somewhere in the Bahamas with her risk-taking, detective uncle on a mission she can't even talk about."

Andrew bit his lip to keep himself from saying more. He had previously admired Amber's ability to gently pry the truth out of someone till she reached the bottom of a matter. Now, he wasn't quite so sure if he enjoyed it very much when the tables were turned on himself.

Amber wisely held her peace and started to scratch tic-tac-toe on a scrap piece of paper.

"Lunch is here!" Steven's voice called to the group as he and Kim appeared, carrying the bags of subs.

Matt and Amber sprang to their feet, while Jimmy and Andrew remained seemingly engrossed in their work.

After a few moments, Kim walked over. "Foot long ham sandwich on wheat with honey mustard for you, Jimmy," she said. "Andrew, here's yours."

"What's on mine?" Andrew teased.

"Whatever Steve ordered for you."

"Thanks, Kim," Jimmy said, trying to prevent Andrew from instigating an argument.

"You're welcome," she smiled. "See, Andrew, at least Jimmy has manners."

"That's because he knows what's on his sub. Mine's mystery meat for all I know."

Kim rolled her eyes.

"Hey Steve, Kim says you made mine a veggie sub with hot peppers. Why would you do something like that to a friend?"

"I said nothing of the sort!" Kim retorted. "Andrew's being a smart-mouth."

Steven laughed. "Knock it off you two. We're going to be seeing a lot of each other these next few days, so let's try to get along."

They were half way through their lunch when Steven's cell phone chirped. The call lasted only a minute, but he had a wide smile on his face when he flipped the phone shut.

"Well, guess who that was," he said. "That sister of mine has arrived in the Bahamas."

"Did you tell her about our change of plans?" Amber asked.

"No. She sounded like she was in a hurry. Besides, it'll be fun to surprise her. Nassau's a relatively small island. We might run into each other."

"What would your uncle say to that?" Andrew asked.

Steven frowned. "I don't know, but he won't be able to do much about it. If we run into each other, I'm sure everything will look casual enough to please him."

"With these rowdy girls?" Jimmy asked with a grin.

"Jimmy!" Kim exclaimed. "I'd expect something like that from Andrew – not from you."

Amber laughed. "I don't care what you say, Steve. Abby and her uncle will be in for a surprise.

— — — — — — — — — — — — — —

As Abby neared the house, she worried her face would betray her. Her eyes felt puffy, and the memory of her angry tears still warmed her face. She knew her face was an open book – Andrew used to tell her that all the time. She would never tell Rick that she had overhead him, and the last thing she wanted to do was lie.

Abby need not have worried. The Bahamian sun was ironically on her side.

The minute she and Freddy stepped into the kitchen, she met the lady she assumed to be Coby's mother, who immediately started chiding her about going out in the sun without a hat.

"You look so hot and red around the eyes already," she fussed, nearly shoving a glass of ice water into her hands.

Abby mumbled her thanks and climbed onto a bar stool to watch the woman busily hustle about the kitchen.

She was a big woman with rough mannerisms, but she was all mother. Her slightly grayed hair was tied up in a tight bun and rested like a crown on top of her head. The frizzy strands that managed to slip out of place seemed a great trial to her. In Mrs. Ward's world, life was meant to be kept neat and in order.

It was only too apparent that Freddy did not quite meet this expectation. His shirt was untucked and his blue jean shorts were showing signs of wear. He was all boy, and Abby smiled at the thought of how they must get along.

Abby herself was hardly the model of put-togeth-erness, but Mrs. Ward seemed to excuse her this once. After all, she was her guest.

"And I haven't even introduced myself," she said. "I'm Mrs. Ward. My boys call me Straw Mamma, 'cause I work at the market.

"And you must be Miss Abigail. Coby told me you were coming, but I thought you'd be a mite smaller. Bless my soul, I was tickled to hear I'd have Rick's niece for company. With five boys, not counting my man, a woman can lose her wits sometimes.

"But I'm just gabbing away, and there's not time now. Eat this," she said, handing Abby a plate of cold cuts and fruit. "I hear your uncle and Coby are talking about going somewhere, and from the sound of things, they're planning to take you with them."

Abby knew it was pointless to argue, and even though she didn't feel hungry, she obliged. But before she had even touched the cold cuts, Mrs. Ward reappeared with a small, well-shaped, colorful straw hat and a bottle of sun lotion.

"You Americans always underestimate our sun. I swear, in the mornings, all the tourists look white. By afternoon, they're as red as Indians."

Thanking her and excusing herself, Abby accepted the lotion and hat and hurried to her room. She was still in no state to see her uncle.

As bidden, she coated herself with a layer of sun-screen, changed back into her Bermuda shorts, and tucked her camera into her purse. All the while, her mind whirled. She knew she couldn't loiter upstairs much longer. She had to face Rick – with a smile.

She turned to her balcony and allowed herself one more minute.

"God, I can't do this myself," she whispered. "I know I'm just as stubborn as Rick is, but he just doesn't understand me, because he doesn't know you.

"I don't know why I'm here since apparently I'm just a convenient carry-on to him. But here I am anyway."

She closed her eyes for a moment and breathed in the thick, humid air. She didn't feel ready, but she knew she had to face her uncle and act as if she hadn't overheard anything.

With a deep breath, she walked back into her room, shut the door to the balcony, grabbed her purse and headed for the stairs.

She felt surprisingly calm descending the stairs. Coby, Rick and Freddy were waiting at the base.

"There you are, Abby," he said. "I thought Freddy had kidnapped you or something. Anyway, I'm glad you've met. Coby and I are going into town and wanted you two to come along."

Abby smiled in agreement, not trusting her voice. Freddy whooped. Apparently, his qualms about baby-sitting had all disappeared.

From behind, Mrs. Ward appeared. "Where are you boys off to?"

"I'm checking in on the boats. One of the guys said there's a buzz of activity going on at Potter's Cay," Coby said. "There are lots of rumors flying about some unusual happenings going on at Cat Island, one of the outer islands. I'm going to drop off

Rick, Abby and Freddy by the water taxis. We'll be home for a late supper."

"Water taxis?" Abby whispered to Freddy.

"To Paradise Island," he explained. "You'll like it. It's a really uptown place that has the largest man-made aquarium in the world."

The four were on their way, but this time, it was apparent that Abby was not the only one who had not enjoyed the cramped quarters in Coby's truck. She and Freddy were delegated to the back of the pick-up.

The bed was dirty and uncomfortable, but Freddy uncovered an old seat cushion that the two managed to share. The ride to Nassau would have been unbearably bumpy but for the cushion – and mercilessly hot without Mrs. Ward's hat.

Abby forgot her worries as they approached Nassau, the capital of the Bahamas located on New Providence Island. Shops soon lined both sides of the road, and Abby was surprised by the selection, which ranged from street side t-shirt vendors to jewelry stores and everything in between.

But what most surprised her was how quickly Nassau changed. One moment, she was passing an expensive shop; the next, graffiti scrawled onto an old building.

It wasn't quite what she had imagined, and yet, it was so new and interesting that she didn't care.

"Look to your left, Abby," Freddy said.

She did so and nearly gasped in delight. The buildings no longer blocked the water's view. They were nearing the water taxis. Freddy pointed out the large cruise ships docked at Price George Wharf and explained how their arrival brought fresh life to Nassau every day.

But Abby wasn't listening. Her eyes had swept past the cruise liners to twin towers that seemed stamped into the landscape beyond. Their peach color reflected the sun's rays brilliantly and made the rest of the horizon pale in comparison. Even from the distance, she could make out their carefully crafted and elaborate architecture.

Freddy smiled. "Those are the Royal Towers of the Atlantis Resort. They are something to look at from a distance and quite another something to see up close. I can't wait to show you around."

Coby was just pulling up in front of the water taxis, and Rick hopped out to buy tickets. Abby jumped down and frowned at the overloaded taxi that waited to depart.

"I think we'll have to wait for the next one," she said to Coby.

He laughed his deep laugh. "No, they'll squeeze you in like sardines. I'll wager they'll manage to get another ten to twelve people on board."

Abby frowned doubtfully, but when the man waiting by the boat saw Rick, he motioned for him to board.

"Catch you later, Coby," he called to his friend and ushered Abby toward the water's edge with Freddy following close behind.

She was squeezed between Freddy and a rather stout woman who was perspiring heavily. The air felt stale under the boat's canopy, and Abby hoped the men would shove off without taking any more passengers.

After accepting another two passengers, they were off. The sea breeze brushed her cheeks as Abby stared across the water to the island, which grew larger and larger. She could barely make out the dialogue of their guide over the boat's engine, and besides, she had Freddy talking into her ear anyway.

His dialogue consisted mostly of gossip about local famous people and eligible bachelors, and she really did not care. Rick grinned at her, and Abby managed to smile back. At least she did not have to attempt conversation.

She still was not even sure why they were making this trip, but Abby knew her uncle was not taking her along with him for her pleasure. She tried not to think about the fact that Rick had intentionally not included her in his "private" conversation with Coby. Some assistant she would make. With the rate her day was going, her "report" to Edith Brightly would be a stretch of her creative writing skills.

"Did you catch that, Abby?" Rick asked. "Look right, and you'll see the water tower – the tallest point on the island."

Abby followed his lead and tried paying harder attention to the guide's recitation. Her uncle was going out of his way to be fatherly, and she knew that he wanted to blend in with the rest of the tourists as much as possible. Her and Freddy's presence certainly made him appear more natural and less like a no-nonsense detective.

The boat docked and its company spilled onto the sidewalks of Paradise Island. A vendor had camped his wares under the bridge that connected the island with New Providence, and Abby stalled just long enough to pick a fabric shoulder bag with colorful hats printed on its sides.

"Don't I look authentic?" she teased Freddy, who had impatiently waited for her to make up her mind between the hat print and another bag with sail boats.

"You women just can't pass up a chance to shop," he grumbled and pointed at Rick who was several yards ahead of them.

"He seems in a hurry," Abby said, jogging to catch up.

"Well, if you want to tour the aquarium, we'd better hurry," Freddy said. "It closes at 5 p.m. That only gives us a little less than two hours."

"Is Rick coming with us?" Abby asked.

"Probably not," Freddy said but offered no other information.

Abby wondered how much he knew about their real purpose in Nassau – and how much he had heard about her.

But for a moment, Abby pushed aside her worries. She was entirely taken in by the beauty – and extravagance – of Paradise Island. High-end shopping and elegant restaurants lined the path leading to the Atlantis Resort, and to her delight, she even caught sight of a Starbucks.

"It feels like home now," she grinned at Rick.

"Maybe on the way back," he smiled and continued at a casual, but brisk, pace.

Royal palms, hibiscus blooms on rambling bushes and the sparkling ocean nearby created the ambiance of a paradise. Children skipped on the brick walkways and pleaded with parents for ice cream from a stand nearby. Lovers embraced on shady verandas, and elderly couples sipped beverages and conversed while watching the activity on the street.

Abby felt as though she were part of the atmosphere, a prop that everyone was used to seeing but had in reality never seen before. The number of tourists made her feel like just that – a number, and she realized that perhaps the myriad of tourists would prove to be Rick's best cover yet.

Meanwhile, Freddy had begun talking to her, and she suddenly realized she had not heard a word.

"I'm sorry, Freddy, you were saying?" she asked, finally bringing her wandering eyes to meet his face.

"I was just asking if you wanted me to take your picture," he said.

"Oh, yes," Abby said, handing him her camera. She leaned against a railing overlooking the water and smiled. Rick watched with an amused look on his face.

"Won't you join me?" she pretended to plead.

"I might break the camera."

"It's a risk I'm willing to take."

"Why don't I just get you and Freddy?" Rick asked.

Freddy was about to hand him the camera when a voice from behind said, "Permit me."

Abby turned to face a middle-aged man. He was wearing a full brim, floral-colored straw hat.

"Well, all right," Rick frowned and threw an arm around Abby's shoulder.

"Thanks so much," Abby said as the man handed her back her camera.

"My pleasure. It's always good to see a family together."

"Oh, we're not family," Freddy laughed.

The man's bronzed face cracked a smile. "Well, you certainly act like one."

Something in the man's voice affirmed Abby's theory about being a prop on a staged set, but she managed to say, "Thanks just the same."

A couple minutes later, she found herself inside the resort, which was brimming with more shops, lounges, restaurants and crowds of people.

Past the shops was an enormous room that housed the casino and led to the hotel and aquarium, as Freddy explained. Rick guided the way through the casino, and Abby, without much success, tried not to stare.

Rows and rows of slot machines flashed on either side, while guests sat mesmerized in front of the screens or pooled in groups at one of the tables or the bar.

Abby had never been inside a casino before and wondered how her uncle would act. He seemed quite at home in the atmosphere and even stopped to ask how someone's game was going. All she could see was the waste – the money and time lost by people glued to screens that flashed numbers, symbols and colors.

Inadvertently, she breathed a sigh of relief when the casino gave way to the hotel lobby. From floor to ceiling, the place seemed like a palace. High ceilings decorated with ornate artwork loomed above them, while polished marble floors lay below.

Abby wanted a chance to take in the atmosphere, but Rick was in a hurry – in a hurry to get rid of her for a while, it seemed. He was already talking with someone at the ticket counter, purchasing passes to the aquarium for Freddy and her.

"You're not coming with us?" she asked.

"Not this time," he smiled. "You run along now and have a good time. I'll meet you back here in two hours."

"Thanks, Mr. Benton," Freddy said, grabbed Abby's hand and turned to enter the aquarium tour. Abby followed but turned her head just in time to see her uncle disappear beyond a staircase.

"Guided tour starts in fifteen minutes," Abby heard someone tell Freddy. "Or, you can explore on your own."

"Thanks, we'll just take a look ourselves," Freddy said. To Abby, he whispered, "I know enough about this aquarium to give my own personal tour."

Abby could only smile. Freddy was enjoying his task of babysitting more than he would ever care to admit.

She soon learned there were many exhibits to the Atlantis aquarium. There was the Dig for viewing a wide array of marine wildlife and several lagoons for viewing reef inhabitants or predators or stingrays.

Just when she thought they had seen it all, Freddy guided her outside the resort toward a mushroomed pavilion that served as both a restaurant and entrance to yet another exhibit.

"You're going to love this," Freddy said. "There's an underwater tunnel."

"A what?"

"Just wait and see," he grinned, leading her down a staircase. When they reached the bottom, the air was cold and wet, and Abby actually wished she had a light jacket.

"Look up," Freddy said.

Abby gasped in surprise and delight. The ceiling of the "mushroom" was a mural of sea life bursting with color.

A tour group was descending the stairs, and Freddy motioned to continue. He was most decidedly not of a crowd mentality.

Abby hurried to keep up with him but in doing so, nearly tripped on a loose shoelace. Another tour group was exiting the entrance to the tunnel, and Abby motioned for Freddy to keep going.

Retreating back toward the staircase, Abby found a bench in front of the floor to ceiling transparent glass that stood between her and thousands of pounds of water and marine life. She turned away from the group and reached down to tie her shoe.

The group's voices echoed off the walls.

"Mommy, I'm hungry. I want something to drink."

"I thought this tour wasn't going to require so much walking."

"Ugg, I hate to go back out into that murderous humidity."

"That tour guide is kind of hot."

"Have you spotted them yet?"

"Look at that stingray!"

"Can you take our picture?"

Abby stood up, only to realize that the last question had been addressed to her. A woman in her late twenties stood smiling and holding out a digital camera. She motioned to the man behind her.

"Oh, sure," Abby said, accepting the camera. She waited till most of the group had passed so she could get a clean shot.

"Thanks," the woman said, grabbed the man's hand and hurried to catch up with their group.

Abby turned toward the tunnel when she noticed a man lingering behind the group. He was talking on a cell phone with his back to her and looking through the glass screen. He was wearing a white polo shirt with blue jeans, and his blond hair was barely visible underneath his baseball cap.

"No, I haven't spotted them," he was saying in a muffled tone. "Don't give me that. You have their descriptions. Besides, you said you saw her yourself, remember?"

Abby froze. She knew that voice. That self-conceited voice.

"You're breaking up," he continued. "No, I haven't seen Benton either, but Ralston has. He thinks Benton's on to the Russians. We can't have our clients thinking our cover is blown."

The tunnel was only feet away, and Abby knew that if she didn't make her exit now, she would be spotted. She casually turned and walked through the tunnel's entrance until she could no longer hear or see him.

Then, she took off running, if for no reason other than to burn off the steam that was clouding her emotions.

What was Neil doing here? Of course, she knew the answer. She just didn't want to believe it. It was too real. He was too close. And all fingers pointed to him as the man responsible for her own close call and as the mastermind behind the plot her uncle was trying to thwart. He had even mentioned Rick's name.

She slowed her pace as she neared yet another group of tourists. She had all but slid past when she recognized yet another man who seemed to be staring at her. He was wearing the same floral full brim hat that the man who had taken their picture half an hour ago had been wearing.

In that moment, she recognized him from somewhere else. He had the same peppered hair, bronzed face and thick build as the man who had been staring at her on the plane to the Bahamas. In short, he was the man behind the newspaper.

Abby turned away and slid between the tourists, ignoring the rules of courtesy. She knew herself well enough. She knew that if he saw her eyes, he'd know what she was thinking.

Freddy was watching barracuda and hammerheads swimming overhead when she found him.

"Hey, where have you been? Check this out!"

"How do we get out of here?" Abby asked, grabbing his arm.

"Whoa, what's going on?"

"He's here – they're here. Now where's the exit?"

She didn't know how much Freddy knew, but he understood. The smile faded from his face.

"We have to go back," he said. "There's only the one exit. We can go in circles for a while, but we have to go out the same way we came in."

Abby frowned and then pulled Freddy out of the walkway into a corner. "Listen, they haven't seen you yet. If we split up, one of us has a better chance of warning Rick."

"About what?"

"Neil said something about Russians and risking getting their cover blown. I don't know what it means, but it must be important, or they wouldn't be looking for us – or Rick."

"But I'm supposed to watch you," he argued. Abby rose and looked behind him.

"Babysitting responsibility is temporarily withdrawn," she said and took off running. Before Freddy could say anything, a man came racing around the corner after her, failing even to notice him.

He paused for only a moment before quickly walking in the opposite direction toward the group of tourists.

He knew the safest thing to do would be to blend in. It wouldn't be the fastest solution, but it would be the least conspicuous.

Each minute feeling like an hour, he made his way through the tour with the group until they returned to the stairs. After ascending to the top, he glanced around him.

Abby was nowhere in sight, and neither was the man in the flowered hat that had been chasing her.

He still had an hour before he and Abby were supposed to rendezvous with Rick, and he didn't have the least idea where to begin looking for him. But he did know where his brother worked in the Atlantis Resort.

Throwing caution to the wind, he took off running toward the main lobby. He arrived breathless, and the clerk looked curiously at him.

"I need to speak with Jacob Ward," he panted.

The clerk raised a disdainful eyebrow and informed him that Mr. Ward was not available at the moment.

"It's important," Freddy insisted.

"I'm sorry, but he's on a tour with a prospective client. You may wait for him in the lobby if you like." With that, the man turned his back on him and busied himself with a pile of papers.

"When will he be back?" Freddy persisted.

Without even turning to look at him, the man replied, "An hour or so."

Seeing that this was getting him nowhere, Freddy decided to play up a fresh angle. Lip trembling, he stammered barely above a whisper, "It's a family emergency."

For the first time, the clerk appeared to take him seriously.

"Look here, you're related to Ward?"

Without looking up, Freddy nodded. "I'm his youngest brother."

"What's the matter?"

Without hesitating, he blurted, "Sister's gone missing."

"I'll page him," the clerk said. "Now just wait over there by those chairs."

Freddy obeyed and chose a seat in the corner, where he could "people watch." Faces seemed to blur together, but he kept his watch. After what seemed like hours, he spotted his brother descending some stairs. He nearly fell out of his seat when he saw Rick right next to him and realized that the "client" the clerk had spoken of was none other than Mr. Benton.

Rick glanced down, spotted Freddy and whispered something to Jacob. After shaking his companion's hand, he turned to talk to the clerk, completely ignoring the boy waiting anxiously just feet away.

Jacob took his cue from the clerk and headed for Freddy, while Rick complained about the inconvenience of having his tour cut short.

The clerk, anxious to please, promised that Rick could return the following day for another complimentary tour and preview of the beaches and attractions off-limits to non-guests. After stiffly thanking the clerk, he walked away toward the casino entrance.

"What gives?" Freddy whispered to his brother, after Rick had walked away without acknowledging him.

"Business, of course," Jacob said. "Now, what's wrong?"

Freddy played up his emotions while the clerk observed, and Jacob returned to explain the situation as vaguely as possible. He received permission to clock off early and then turned to walk through the casino.

They found Rick sitting at a slot machine at the far end.

"What's going on?" he demanded of Freddy. "You nearly blew our cover."

"I didn't know where you were, so I went to find Jake," he defended himself. "How was I supposed to know you two were together on this?"

"That's beside the point," Rick sighed. "Where's Abby?"

As quickly as possible, Freddy recounted the story and then waited for Rick's response. His face turned grave.

"I know a couple of the guys who work here," Jacob offered. "I could get them looking for her."

"Not good," Rick shook his head. "If El GATO is daring enough to plan an abduction in broad daylight, they're getting desperate. I don't want to generate any more heat. They obviously know we're here. If they're worried we'll spook the Russians, the last thing we need to do is create a sensation about a missing person.

"Remember, we don't want to frighten away these Russian clients either," Rick said. "If they fly the coop, we're left with no evidence that El GATO is marketing a potentially dangerous substance. We'll have no chance to nab them in the act."

"Then what are we going to do?" Freddy asked impatiently.

"Nothing," Rick said, his jaw set.

"But she's your niece!" Freddy protested.

"Keep it down," Jacob warned him. "We've got at least seven of us to look for her, between our family and Mr. Benton."

Rick turned to Freddy and placed a reassuring hand on his shoulder. In a distant voice, he said, "This isn't personal; it's business. El GATO is one up in this round. They were more brazen than I had anticipated, and that's regretful.

"But Abby's capable, and even if she did fall into their hands, she's a bargaining chip. They're not going to hurt her – or seriously hurt her – just yet."

Freddy was speechless. He couldn't believe that he appeared to care more for this young woman whom he had met just over an hour ago than her own uncle, who was seemingly indifferent to the fact she may have been abducted.

Freddy finally found his voice. "And if that's the case? And they try to use her as a bargaining chip?"

"Then I'll try my hand at roulette," Benton said with a wry smile.

Chapter 11

Afternoon Escapade

Abby did not have to run far before encountering a second large group of tourists admiring the underwater exhibit. Here was her chance.

"Snake!" she shrieked as loudly as she could. It was the first thing that came to her mind and the last of her concerns, but her ploy worked.

Women started shrieking in return and generating a lot of confusion, while the men tried to reason with them as to the improbability of a snake in an under-water tunnel.

In short, a miniature version of pandemonium broke out, giving Abby the chance to sneak toward the stairs and make her exit.

She wasn't sure when she had lost her pursuer, but by the time she reached the outside, he wasn't behind her.

Nearly breathless, she continued jogging away from the building with the mushroom-shaped roof until she found a small outside vendor brimming with tourists. She walked to the counter, bought a large lemonade, and sat down under a small umbrella in a secluded spot.

She had a perfect view of the mushroomed pavilion and would have plenty of time to spot Neil or the man in the flowered hat before they would notice her.

Her breath began to come easier, and she paused to sip her lemonade. She needed to think. She needed to meet up with Rick and Freddy in half an hour. Rick would know what to do next.

She had been so unprepared to see Neil and then alarmed at the brazen attempt made by the man in the flowered hat. Apparently, whomever she was against was desperate and not afraid to take risks.

A voice behind her caught her attention. She turned to see a man two tables across from her who was wearing a light blue polo shirt and talking on a cell phone. He had dark hair, an olive complexion and what struck Abby as a disproportionate face: small nose, big ears, large brow, and sensitive eyes.

What struck her even more was the nature of his dialogue.

"What do you mean she got away?" He demanded with a well-defined New York accent. "I thought Kurt was going to take care of the kid, and you and I were going to meet our clients at the shop?"

Was he talking about her? Abby slid lower into her seat and felt her face grow warm. Was Kurt the man in the flowered hat?

"How am I supposed to know what she looks like?" he muttered. "Half the girls around here have brown hair, brown eyes, and rich uncles.

"Forget the girl for all I care. I'm going to take the water taxi back to Nassau and be on time for our appointment. Sure, I'll tell them you were detained, but you'd better be there when they start talking business."

He flipped his phone shut, shoved the chair back and walked to the counter. "Put it on the tab."

"Of course, Mr. Ralston," the man said, as the man called Ralston walked away.

Abby didn't have time to think. She knew she didn't have time to meet Freddy and Rick at their scheduled rendezvous if she wanted to follow this man.

And yet, she had no way to communicate with them that she was fine.

It was a risk she felt she had to take.

Lemonade in hand, she began to casually follow the man from a distance, all the while her heart pounding.

She glanced down at her Bermuda shorts and frowned. What if Neil or Kurt met Ralston at the water taxis? She would be easily recognized.

She passed a small vendor selling cover-ups and fabric hats and felt for her wallet. She was sure the wares would be overpriced, and yet, desperate times called for desperate measures.

Taking one last look at Ralston who was still walking down the road toward the bridge, she paused long enough to select a coral-colored cover-up, white flowing hat and the largest pair of sunglasses available.

The cover-up was long enough to hide her shorts, with terry cloth sleeves that covered the thin straps of her tank top. Cramming Mrs. Ward's straw hat into the bag she had purchased earlier, she slipped the hat on and slid the glasses over her nose.

There. Now she looked just like every other sunburned woman walking down the road toward the taxis.

Skipping to catch up with a group of middle-aged women, she craned her neck to catch a glimpse of Ralston. He was nowhere in sight.

She knew the water taxi left every half hour, Bahama time. If Bahama time were on her side, Ralston would still be waiting for a taxi by the time she reached the dock.

She needn't have worried. He was impatiently talking on his cell phone and pacing the pier as the taxi appeared in sight.

After handing the man the ticket her uncle had purchased for the return ride, she hustled next to some of the other ladies. Ralston was hardly visible over the array of hats and bodies that crammed once again into the taxi.

Abby didn't think he would notice her above all the other women but couldn't help but wonder why he kept looking in her direction.

Then, she knew.

A man a couple seats down had started singing. People started pointing, snickering, and laughing, and Abby realized he was drunk.

"No more pain, no more drama in my life!" He sang with abandon in a slurred voice. "No more pain! No more drama! In my life!"

Competing for attention was the taxi guide, who was patiently trying to point out tourist attractions, flirt with the women on board, and tell a couple jokes.

But the drunk was clearly stealing the show. No one even noticed the young woman in the coral cover-up who exited the taxi by herself, lingered a few moments by the waterside to rummage through her bag, and then casually began to shadow a well-dressed man down Bay Street.

Abby followed from a safe distance but had a hard time keeping up with Ralston's brisk pace. He crossed the busy street, and she hesitated. She didn't think he was suspicious of her yet, but she didn't want to take any chances.

A man like Ralston would know when he was being followed.

Instead of crossing the street, she continued to saunter along the sidewalk, glancing into shop front windows and feigning interest in the wares of street side vendors while keeping her eye on the man in the blue polo shirt.

"Buy shirts three for ten," a man beside her offered. Abby glanced at him to shake her head and then looked back across the street.

Ralston had disappeared.

Her heart pounded. He couldn't have gone far. Maybe he had entered a shop. Directly across the street were another t-shirt vendor and a jewelry store called South American Treasures.

She watched for traffic before jogging across the street and entering the jewelry store, which was surprisingly busy.

To her relief, half the other women in the shop were wearing cover-ups or other beach attire, so she did not feel out of place. However, most had removed their sunglasses to gaze into the glass cases.

Reluctantly, she pulled hers off and clipped them to her bag, reassuring herself that Ralston couldn't possibly recognize her since he didn't know what she looked like.

She spied a man silhouetted against the shop's back door. His height matched Ralston's, but his back was turned toward her. He appeared to be talking with someone in an adjacent room. She had to get a better look.

As she inched her way to the back of the store, she realized there was no way to access the back of the shop without getting behind the counter, which swarmed with salesmen.

"May I help you, Ma'am?" a woman's voice addressed her.

Abby smiled warmly. "Yes, I was just admiring that emerald ring there. That's right, the one shaped like a flower."

"It's a favorite," the woman replied. "Would you like to try it on?"

"Please," Abby said. As the woman unlatched the glass case, Abby chanced a look toward the back. The tall man – if he were Ralston – had disappeared, and her heart sank. She had no way of telling if he were her man, or just another salesman.

"What a wild goose chase this is turning out to be," she thought to herself.

"Here you are," the woman said.

"Oh, it's lovely," Abby said, "and just my size. How much is it?"

"That one is $350, but have you heard about our special?"

Abby listened patiently, all the while admiring the ring.

"Well, I really should talk it over with George," she said, reluctantly handing it back to the saleswoman. "How late are you open?"

"Until six," she replied. "And when you do come back, make sure you ask for me. My name is Katherine."

"Thank you, Katherine," Abby smiled once again. She was just about to turn around when she saw Katherine look past her and smile broadly. The look told her that the saleswoman recognized someone standing right behind her.

Abby pretended to stare into another glass case as Katherine moved past her.

"This way, Sir," she heard the saleswoman say. "Your clients are waiting for you."

"Is Ralston here yet?" she heard a familiar voice whisper.

"Yes, Sir," she replied in equally subdued tones.

The man brushed past her to follow Katherine behind the counter, and Abby could feel her knees grow weak.

The man had been so close she could smell his cologne. His arm had brushed the back of her bag.

And by the sound of his voice, Abby knew that the man was none other than Neil DeWitt.

Abby glanced up in time to see Neil disappear into the back room. Katherine was returning.

The shop was filled with tourists, and Abby knew that if she attempted a quick retreat, she would create a stir. Abby had no choice but to put on a brave face and attempt a final smile at Katherine who seemed to be watching her as she walked slowly through the crowd to exit the shop.

Katherine smiled back.

Abby hoped her face had not betrayed her heart.

Outside the shop, she felt her face grow hot and realized how tired and thirsty she was – and how close she had been to meeting Neil face to face again.

The danger was real, and now every man wearing a hat seemed to look like the man named Kurt who had chased her so brazenly in the aquarium.

She needed to think what to do next. It was too late to return to Paradise Island and try to find Rick and Freddy. By now, they could already be back at the Ward's house.

How far away was the Ward's house? Could she find it herself? She didn't even know what their house number was.

At that moment, she realized how much Rick was trying to shelter her. He hadn't planned for her to be out of his or Freddy's or Coby's sight for even a moment.

She didn't know how much Rick knew about the deal that was about to go down at South American

Treasures or about the Russians or about Neil being in Nassau.

But she knew that time was short, and she needed to alert him as soon as possible.

She reached into her purse and pulled out her wallet. She did have a phone card. If only she knew where to find a public phone.

A local directed her to the closest one, and she dialed the one number she knew – other than her home number.

After all, she hadn't spent last summer as the front desk receptionist at Drake and Benton for nothing.

— — — — — — — — — — — — — —

Rick's nerves were on edge. Freddy hadn't stopped his doomsday forecasting the entire afternoon. Jacob Ward had no luck searching for Abby. Coby had alerted his brother down at Potter's Cay to keep an eye open but with no results.

Even his own discreet inquiries had turned up nothing. No one had seen a young woman wearing Bermuda shorts, tank top, and straw hat accompanied by a man in a flowered hat.

Or at least, no one had noticed.

"What will Mom say?" Freddy's voice interrupted his thoughts.

The mention of Mrs. Ward made Rick wince at the thought of his own sister Michelle. How would she react if she heard that her daughter were missing, presumed kidnapped?

He pushed the thought aside. The situation was critical but required no immediate action. If El GATO were behind Abby's disappearance, it was their turn to play a hand before he made his move.

Coby pulled into his driveway, and Freddy jumped out of the truck's bed before they had come to a complete stop. He took off running toward the back of the house without saying another word.

Rick looked over at Coby, who said, "Don't worry about Freddy. He's just young and impressionable. It looks like he's taken quite a notion to your niece and probably feels responsible – or angry with us.

"He'll let off some steam and come back to the house when he's ready."

Rick nodded. "I'm not worried."

"About Freddy or Abby?"

"I'm trying not to worry about either of them," he said slamming his door shut. "Abby wasn't born yesterday. She may be young, but she has her wits about her – most of the time."

"Well I'm worried," Coby replied. "Wits or no wits, it seems like everyone who's looked closely into this business, specifically, its island connections, has either had some close calls or dropped off the map."

"I just wish I knew what she heard about Russians," Rick changed the subject. "Freddy doesn't tell the story very coherently."

"Freddy's emotional. He'll get over it."

The two stepped onto the doorstep and parted ways at the stairs.

"I'm going to check in with some of the fellows at the boats. Maybe they've heard something concrete regarding the rumors about Cat Island being a hot spot right now. I'll be back around seven for supper," Coby said and headed for the back door.

Rick nodded and mounted the first step. He needed to call Owens and Brightly.

He was just about to turn the knob to his room when he heard water running. It was coming from the room across from his. Abby's room.

He hesitated before walking across the hall and knocking on the door. There was no answer.

The door wasn't locked, so he creaked it open and peaked inside. A coral-colored cover up and some other clothes had been tossed onto the bed, and Abby's suitcase was flung open.

The sound of running water was coming from her bathroom.

"Hello?" he called cautiously. He paused to listen. Someone was singing in the shower.

"Abby?" he ventured, opening the bathroom door an inch.

"Rick!" he heard his niece shriek. "Close the door! I'll be out in a minute."

He blinked in surprise and quickly pulled the door shut. He heard water running for a few more moments, then the curtain slide, then something drop.

He turned his back to the door and leaned against it, heart pounding. All he felt was an overwhelming sense of intense relief. She was here, and she was safe.

"Thank God," he muttered and headed for his room.

— — — — — — — — — — — — — — —

Abby met the whole Ward clan that evening. Coby was the oldest, and in addition to Freddy, there were three other brothers: Jacob, Warren, and AJ. Mr. Ward was a friendly man in his sixties, and although technically retired, he still worked with his sons who had taken over his fishing business.

Warren and AJ also worked the boats, and Abby guessed that Coby's fishing "job" was primarily a front for his undercover work.

No wonder Mrs. Ward was excited to have a "woman's company." Being surrounded by five men, their adolescent brother, and her uncle made her feel like a minority.

To her amusement, she held them captive with the account of her afternoon adventure. Mrs. Ward clucked her tongue disapprovingly when Abby told the group about following the man named Ralston to the water taxies.

"If I was you, I would've gone straight the other way," she said.

Coby grinned at Rick. "That strikes me as something you might do yourself."

"What happened next?" Warren asked, eyes gleaming. He was the largest of the brothers, towering even over Coby. His muscles rippled under his shirt, but he seemed like another gentle giant.

She glanced at her uncle who nodded, and she resumed. Rick trusted the Ward family, so she saw no cause not to do the same. After all, Coby's brothers had gathered gossip from the docks, cluing in Jacob of the rumors surrounding the Russian clientele at the Atlantis Resort. From there, he had done his homework and reported back to Coby.

It was almost like having an espionage ring within one family.

"Wish I could have gone with you," Freddy mumbled.

"Of course you do," AJ winked at Abby.

Mrs. Ward cleared the table as Warren went to fetch some card games. Abby caught her uncle's eye and coughed lightly before nodding toward the family room.

Rick took the hint. "Mrs. Ward, will you excuse us for a moment?"

"Thanks so much for supper," Abby added. "It was delicious."

"Well, hurry back," AJ called. "I want to see how well you play." He winked at her again.

Coby followed Rick and Abby to the living room. "There are just a couple more things I want to tell you, and I have my share of questions for you."

"That's putting it straight enough," Coby laughed.

"Well?" Rick asked. "I'm listening."

Abby took a deep breath and plunged in. "I just don't feel like you're being very square with me – not telling me things and not trusting me very much. I hope I can prove I'm worth trusting.

"After I followed Ralston into the shop, I waited around a bit. I really felt that somewhere in the back room he was talking with the Russians. When Ralston was talking on his cell phone back at Paradise Island, he mentioned something about making sure to be on time for an appointment.

"I think that appointment was at South American Treasures. I think the shop is being used as a cover for an entirely different operation."

"We're listening," Coby said.

"Well, not long afterward, I was talking to a saleswoman named Katherine, and I noticed her look up as if to make eye contact with someone behind me.

"I was right. She excused herself and stepped forward to meet a man whose voice I recognized."

Abby paused. "That man was Neil DeWitt. I didn't see him. But I recognized his voice. He followed Katherine to the back room."

"Did you see him come back out?" Rick asked.

"No, I felt I might generate some heat if I continued to nose around the shop without actually buying anything," Abby said. "That's when I left and phoned the office to get the Ward's address."

"Do you think anyone grew suspicious of you?" Coby asked. "Was the shop busy?"

"It was pretty busy, and I don't think anyone really noticed me," Abby hesitated.

Rick frowned. "They could have surveillance cameras, and if the shop really is a front, your description should be in everyone's hands by now."

"Your uncle has a point. We're going to need to act fast," Coby said. "First thing tomorrow, I'll send someone to check out the place. My man will know how to get around back. This could be a big break."

For the first time that night, Abby saw Rick smile. "I guess you're going to have some report to type up tonight. But first, shall we join the card game?"

"Won't you tell me your story?" Abby asked. "Who are these Russians, and why are they so important? Why didn't you tell me the real reason you wanted to go to Paradise Island today?"

Rick's smile quickly faded. "You've heard the saying, 'Ignorance is bliss.' Trust me, if you really had been abducted today, you would have been thanking me about now for not telling you anything about my suspicions and my suspects."

Abby bit her lip. "That may be so, but at this point, it's just a little more water under the bridge. Neil knows I'm here and either thinks I know more than I do or that I'm with someone who knows more than he should.

"Remember that the man in the flowered hat – Kurt, I think his name is – was on the same plane we were on earlier today. That could be just a coincidence, but it may not have been."

Coby glanced at Rick as if to acknowledge her point.

"Look, Abby, you're here for several reasons. One, you're my personal assistant. Two, you're good cover – or you were good cover. Three, you're our only witness; you may have handled PS59. You recognized this so-called Kurt on the plane and placed him as the man who chased you today. And, you were able to detect Neil's voice without ever seeing his face.

"So I'll tell you this: the Russians are El GATO's client, and after Coby's and my footwork today, we've learned their stay in the Bahamas is not for mere pleasure. This is business, expensive business. It's the kind of business that means you throw away thousands of dollars in reservations at the Atlantis Resort and barely even spend a couple hours there.

"They're in the market for PS59, and they may or may not be alone. But time is not on El GATO's side. They were detected in Miami, and they know someone is on their scent again."

"You're sure it's El GATO behind all this?" Abby asked.

"Ninety-nine percent sure," Coby said. "The Greater American Terrorist Organization not only instigates acts of terrorism; it also fuels them. Whoever gets his hands on this psycho-stimulant probably does not want to use it to merely pass a physical exam or stay up all night studying.

"We're talking the potential to create a superman, a machine that doesn't need sleep or rest like normal people. Granted, we don't know what kind of rebound or crash the drug causes, but apparently someone knows and is willing to take the risk anyway."

"The short version is, Abby, this case is no child's game," Rick said. "You are a little fish in the big ocean, and these men aren't going to care that you're a sweet young thing. They won't think twice before killing you.

"And that's why, I didn't – and haven't – told you everything I know. You already know enough to be a target; today proves that. We have to be extra careful from now on about where you go and who you're with."

"AJ might offer to baby-sit," Coby teased.

"I don't need babysitting," Abby made a face. "I can help. I want to help."

"Subject closed," Rick stood up. "We'll investigate the shop front tomorrow and go from there. Right now, it's Friday night, and it's time to play some cards."

"I'm going to go type up that report to Edith before she thinks I forgot," Abby sighed, rising as well. "And then I'm going to send up a prayer for tomorrow."

"Send up an SOS for all I care," Rick laughed, following Coby back to the dining room. "It all boils down to luck. You're lucky or not so lucky. And that determines who wins and who loses."

Abby disagreed. "In cards maybe, but not in life."

Chapter 12

Monday Morning

꙰

The sun sparkled as it emerged into the morning sky, causing a dazzling light to reflect off the ocean's surface. It was as if God were dipping an invisible ladle into the ocean's bowl and gently scooping to the surface a golden nugget.

Abby could not help but catch her breath. She was wrapped in a pink bathrobe, barefoot, and leaning against the balcony's railing that was only footsteps away from the guestroom's bed. Her elbows were propped up, hands cupping her chin, fingers rubbing her eyes.

Was she waking up in a fairy tale, or would reality rub off the pixie dust the minute the sun's morning dance had ended?

She glanced down at her pink bathrobe and smiled softly. Was it only a few weeks ago that she had driven to St. Vincent and visited Dixie? Duff's accident, Neil's surprise arrival, her assault in the graveyard, her uncle's surprise job offer, and this trip to the Bahamas seemed unreal.

She had thought the fantasy world in which she seemed to be living was almost at an end, the case almost closed. Her mind had tidied up the whole affair: Rick and Coby were to capture the villains at the jewelry store, whisk them away to jail, and hail her a heroine. She would sip lemonade on the beach and read an Agatha Christie mystery novel to celebrate.

Abby laughed at her own foolishness, but her laugh turned to a sigh. She was foolish and certainly no great heroine. But to realize that all Rick's, Coby's and her footwork had led them nowhere – well, it had not been an easy loss to swallow.

True to his word, Rick had investigated the shop first thing Saturday morning, only to find that someone had "closed shop" overnight. South American Treasures had seemingly gone out of business, and rumors indicated the owners weren't far from Queer Street. Locals accepted the stories of financial problems, and life on Bay Street resumed its normal ebb and flow as tourists poured in from the cruise liners, bringing with them vitality and money to spend.

Strike two fell when Jacob alerted Coby that the alleged Russians rooming at the Atlantis Resort had paid up, checked out, and frankly, escaped all surveillance.

Strike three came when their final lead checked out – negative. Warren and AJ had been hearing snatches of rumors about some unusual activity around Cat Island, and Rick had been tempted to catch a plane to investigate.

But not another word had been whispered about Cat Island since, and Coby was left to assume the excitement had stemmed from the annual Rake 'N' Scrape Music Festival.

It was as if El GATO had vanished into thin air, leaving behind only a memory of its presence. Abby even heard some of the Ward brothers murmur as to whether she had imagined her whole adventure.

She knew Rick believed her, and that's what drove home the reality of their situation. Friday had been a close call for her. But how could El GATO be so brazen one day and virtually disappear the next?

There had been one bright spot to Saturday. Agent Owens passed along an anonymous tip that El GATO was suspected of a rendezvous with a potential PS59 reseller on Little Abaco Island. Since Coby was slipping back into his undercover life as a fisherman in hopes of catching a lead, Rick determined to investigate by himself.

He flatly told Abby that she was to stay put. Abby reflected with a wry smile that she hadn't even had a chance to protest. Rick had called her "their only witness" and swore he would "ground her" before letting her go traipsing off into El GATO's hands.

That had been Saturday afternoon. Freddy had distracted her by dragging her into the backyard beach to play volleyball and swim. It had been an enjoyable pastime – until he decided that Sunday would be spent much the same way. By Sunday evening, she was so sore and sunburned that she was desperately hoping Rick would return by morning or that she would spend all of Monday inside reading.

But now, it was Monday, and the only word she had received from her uncle was a quick text message, saying he was still investigating the lead and probably would not return until Tuesday at the earliest.

That only left them one day until the scheduled sale, but Abby knew she didn't need to remind her uncle of that fact. She knew Rick was well aware that precious time had been lost. Since he was being so tight-lipped about his assignment in Little Abaco, she had no way of knowing if he were back on El GATO's trail or just running in circles.

She wished she could help him. She felt like a prisoner in the Ward's lovely home on a paradise beach in the Bahamas. It was cruelly ironic.

The sun was now well on its way to climbing the morning sky, and Abby arched her back and allowed herself one last look at the morning's beauty. She could hear Mrs. Ward downstairs fixing breakfast and knew that she would be expected to join the family in a few minutes.

She would obey orders. She would allow Freddy to bore her to tears with his ridiculous stories and flattery. Well, he had promised to take her to the Straw Market, so perhaps that would be diverting.

She would lounge on the beach since Rick did not seem to want her to earn her keep as his "assistant."

She would try not to think about Neil out there, somewhere, smiling to himself in satisfaction just as he had done the moment Dixie had opened the front door to him, unaware that she, Abby, had been trying to keep out a villain.

— — — — — — — — — — — — — — —

The minute the island's silhouette appeared through *Wing's* windows, the hull broke into squeals of delight comparable to a middle school class with sixty seconds remaining to summer break.

Andrew pulled his pillow over his head, realizing the futility of trying to shush the sisters. He came up for air, just in time to glance out the window himself. It was hard to believe that somewhere, only miles away, Abby was in the middle of her detective business with her uncle.

Andrew had second-guessed Rick's motives from the start. It seemed to him that Abby's memory had fast faded from her uncle's neglect and ingratitude toward her last summer when she had poured herself into boring office work.

He certainly had his suspicions, and his uneasiness had only grown after their argument. That had been the last time he had talked to her. Abby had not even tried to phone or text him since arriving in the Bahamas.

Matt's voice over the intercom interrupted his thoughts, and in what seemed like no time at all, *Wings* made a smooth landing in the Bahamas.

Ian's friend Lawrence was waiting for them and helped them jump through the required red tape. A team from the church helped unload the cargo supplies for the missionaries, while Matt and Jimmy made arrangements for stowing the plane in a rented hangar.

"We're so glad to have you boys here," Lawrence said, pausing to wipe some sweat off his brow. "And ladies, of course," he smiled at Kim and Amber.

He led the way to the church van, and the group climbed inside, stuffing luggage in wherever it would fit.

"Looks like it's the roof rack for you, Andrew," Steven grinned.

"We'll all fit," Lawrence laughed, starting the engine. "I'm going to drop the girls off at the Browns and swing by your hotel to unload your luggage. The plan is to get you guys settled in and then meet up for supper around 5 o'clock, if that works for you."

"What is for supper?" Andrew called from the very back seat, fanning the air with a full brim hat to get some circulation.

"Always thinking of your stomach," Matt teased.

Lawrence laughed. "The Browns recommended going to one of the local restaurants to give you all a taste of our cuisine. I think the young ladies might appreciate that it's right around the corner from the Straw Market. We might have some time to look around before supper, if anyone's interested."

"Girls interested in shopping? I doubt it," Andrew winked at Kim.

"Don't ever listen to him," she retorted.

"Where have you been holding your church services since the fire?" Steven changed the subject.

"We hold open air tent meetings in the morning," said Lawrence. "Of course, that will soon change once we get the ground breaking started. With the manpower we have and your help, we'll make a fine start tomorrow after the ceremony."

"Well, we're not here for a vacation," Jimmy said. "At least, we guys aren't."

"Don't you start too, Jimmy," Kim scolded. "Alathea says there's going to be plenty for everyone to do, and besides, someone's got to keep you men fed."

"Amen to that," Andrew chimed from the back seat.

— — — — — — — — — — — — — —

"Let's see, we have about two hours left until we're supposed to meet Mom at the Straw Market, so we'd better hurry if I'm going to have time to show you everything," Freddy said, pulling Abby by the hand.

Mrs. Ward had dropped off Freddy and Abby downtown that morning before heading off to work at the Straw Market, and Freddy had proceeded to give her a grand tour of Nassau's attractions. They had already been to Fort Charlotte and the Ardastra Gardens, and by three o'clock, she felt as though she had worn a hole in the bottom of her shoes. She was having a hard time deciding which was worse: shadowing Neil's henchman Friday or keeping up with a fifteen-year-old boy with leather feet.

"Parliament Square to your right," Freddy announced. "English Loyalists built those pink buildings in the early 1800s after moving from North

Carolina to the Bahamas. Nassau is the center of the Bahamian government, with other government buildings in the immediate vicinity."

"Fascinating," Abby said, trying not to sound sarcastic. "Who's that supposed to be?" She pointed toward a statue of a lady, which served as a prominent feature of the square.

"That's Queen Victoria," Freddy answered. "It's a very flattering statue of her, isn't it?"

As flattering as statues go, Abby thought and picked up her pace to keep up with her companion. She could only imagine the subject line for today's daily update to Ms. Edith Brightly: Nassau's Culture, Economy, and Impact on the World.

For the first time all afternoon, Abby felt like smiling. Not because she knew Edith would appreciate the title, but because she was imagining the woman's facial expression upon opening her inbox.

Her recent experience had taught her that this woman had no sense of humor. Abby's Friday report had only received a grudging compliment and a definite scolding for taking such a risk by "her own inexperienced self."

Her report on their disappointment regarding the jewelry shop had actually been received better than she had anticipated. Edith had written a sympathetic note, but its undertone had downplayed her discovery. Abby strongly suspected Edith was behind Rick's definite refusal for her to accompany him to Little Abaco.

"We're nearing our destination," Freddy said.

"Which is?" Abby asked, realizing she had not been paying attention.

"The Queen's Staircase and Fort Fincastle," Freddy replied. "I'm sure you're going to just love the place. You see, if you walk up the Queen's Staircase, you'll find yourself at Fort Fincastle. The fort's water tower is the highest spot on the island, which, I might add, will give you an awesome view."

Abby had had her fill of forts for the day, but as she approached the staircase, her perception changed. The ugly streets and cracked sidewalks gave way to a secluded spot, where the damp air hung like a cool canopy, and towering cliffs of limestone loomed on each side. Vendors dotted the walk to the staircase, and a small waterfall cascaded directly next to the stairs.

"It's lovely," Abby said.

"The Queen's Staircase is named after Queen Victoria," Freddy resumed his dialogue. "You see, the staircase has the same number of steps as the number of years in Victoria's reign."

"And what number is that?" Abby asked, beginning to count the steps as she ascended.

"Sixty-six," Freddy replied.

A moment later, Abby reached the top and called down to Freddy, who was surprisingly a few steps behind her. "I only counted 65."

"That's because your friend told you wrong."

Abby turned toward the voice. An old woman was sitting on a bench next to a welcome sign for the staircase. She had a mass of gray curly hair and large-rimmed glasses, from under which peered intelligent black eyes.

"My nephew once asked the same question himself," she said. "The fact is, Queen Victoria only reigned 65 years, and initially, there were 66 steps to the staircase. However, time and the elements decayed one of the steps, so only the 65 remain today."

"Interesting," Abby murmured, before following Freddy toward Fort Fincastle.

"Stupid tourist," he muttered. "How's she supposed to know more than I do about my own city's backyard?"

Abby felt it wise not to reply. She stole one last glance back toward the staircase exit.

The old woman had disappeared.

— — — — — — — — — — — — — — —

"Those girls are five minutes late," Andrew sighed, glancing at his wristwatch.

"It's probably not their fault," Lawrence said, eyes twinkling. "You have to understand something about time here: There is no 'on time' or 'late' in the Bahamas. There's only Bahama time, and that's how life operates."

"Beats me how anyone gets anything done," Steven said.

"I feel that way sometimes too," Lawrence admitted. "If you guys want to explore the market, go ahead. I'll wait here for the Browns and your girl-friends to arrive."

"Why don't you and Andrew go ahead, Steve," Jimmy agreed. "Matt and I will wait here and catch up with you later. Let's plan to meet up for supper back here around 5:15."

Andrew and Steven didn't argue and welcomed the chance to stretch their legs. Some of the vendors at the Straw Market were already starting to close up for the afternoon, so they wanted to take in what they could.

"From what I've heard, these people are real hagglers," Steven warned.

"I can handle a haggler," Andrew said.

"Well, I've heard that they're downright brazen at times. And besides, it's the end of the day. Some may be desperate for a sale."

"Hey, maybe we'll find something for that sister of yours. You haven't heard from her again, have you?"

"No, just that quick call," Steven said. "I'm trusting that no news is good news."

"Aren't we both," Andrew thought to himself.

Steven and Andrew managed to avoid incident with any of the vendors until they arrived at a rather prominent booth of straw hats.

"Check out this monstrosity!" Andrew joked, pretending to try on a large hat with flowers and fake fruit piled high.

"I'll give it to you for thirteen," a Bahamian woman told Andrew.

"Thirteen?" Andrew couldn't help but laugh.

"Twelve."

"Sorry, not my size," Andrew said, replacing the hat.

"Make it ten," she said, forcing the hat back into Andrew's hands.

Andrew dropped the hat on her counter. "Sorry, it's not my style either."

"Wait! I will make you a bargain!" the heavy woman asserted, stepping in front of Andrew. She blocked the narrow path completely, making it impossible for Andrew to pass.

"Sorry, but I'm not interested," Andrew replied impatiently.

"Please buy," she pleaded. "It has been such a slow day."

"Sorry, but I don't like the hat."

"But it becomes you so!" she insisted. Andrew stared doubtfully at the gaudy fruit and flowers.

"Do you have any bead necklaces?" Steven quickly asked her. "I'd like to get one for my sister."

"I have many," she beamed broadly, finally dropping the hat subject. "Which one do you like?"

Steven decided on one and brought it down in price.

"Thanks," he smiled and turned to Andrew.

"I'll be here again tomorrow if you change your mind about the hat!" she called after Andrew.

"Please," Andrew moaned.

"Let's go find the others," Steven laughed and Andrew readily agreed. "I can't wait to tell them about you and your special lady-friend."

"Spare me," Andrew said. They were just about to turn in the direction of the restaurant when someone caught Andrew's eye.

"Hey Steve, doesn't that girl look like . . . Abby!"

"Where?" Steven asked.

"Standing across the street from that store, the one called South American Treasures."

Steven turned to look at the young woman standing across the street from the jewelry store. She was talking to a teenage boy but kept glancing around her.

"It sure looks like her," Steven said, already starting in her direction. Andrew had to jog to catch up.

"Abby," Steven called to her. She turned to the direction of his voice.

"Steve!" she cried, rushing over to meet him.

"You know him?" Freddy asked, eyeing Steven suspiciously.

Abby laughed. "Freddy, this is my brother. Steve, this is Freddy, a friend of mine."

"Nice to meet you," Freddy frowned, "but what about his friend?"

"What friend?" Abby asked, but no sooner had the words left her mouth than she saw Andrew.

"Just along for the ride," he said, trying to hide a sheepish grin as Abby greeted him with a big hug.

Suddenly, she lowered her voice. "I'm really glad to see you both, honestly, but this isn't the best timing. You see, Freddy and I were just debating whether we should go into that jewelry store when we saw you."

"What's to debate about?" Andrew asked. "It's just a jewelry store. I'm sure you don't have to have reservations."

Freddy interrupted. "Abby, we're supposed to meet Mom in fifteen minutes. If we're going to see if the store is really open again, we'd better be quick about it."

"I have to know," Abby replied. "It was just closed 'for good' as of two days ago. How can it be back in business so soon?"

"This is all very interesting, Abby, but we don't have any idea what you're getting at," Andrew said.

"I can't explain right now, but I might be able to use your help," Abby said, biting her lip in concentration. "You're tall and handsome . . ."

"Well, thank you," Andrew grinned.

"Don't interrupt," Abby scolded. "Can you flirt credibly?"

"Can I what?"

"Flirt – you know," Abby sighed impatiently.

"Your shimmering eyes look bewitching, but your rosy lips speak of nonsense," Andrew played along.

"You'll have to do," Abby said, ignoring his remark. "Okay, I need you to go into that jewelry store, find a clerk named Katherine and distract her while I find a way to get behind the counter."

"Don't tell me you're going to steal something," Andrew was openly alarmed.

"Just trust me on this one. Steve, once Andrew and I have been in the store a few minutes, I need you to create a distraction out front. Anything you can think of will do. And Freddy, see if you can't get around back and keep an open eye. If something happens to me, I need you to get Coby."

"Sis, are you sure about this?" Steven asked.

"It sounds crazy, I know, but please help me on this. I'll plan to meet you all at the Straw Market – in under half an hour."

"I don't think your uncle would like this, Abby," Freddy said.

"But Rick's not here right now, is he?" Abby replied, sliding her bulky sunglasses over her eyes. She turned to Andrew and slipped her arm into his. "Come, Darling, let's go look at diamonds."

Chapter 13

Deception

Katherine Brown looked up into the dark brown eyes of a tall American man and smiled. "Is there something I can help you with, Sir?"

"Shhh," he put a finger to his lips and nodded toward a young woman whose back was turned to them both. She was wearing a sky blue blouse and hunching over one of the glass displays, admiring the jewelry.

"My fiancé and I have a bet going to see who has the best taste and can find the best deal. The rules are that we have to find five pieces per store and compare our finds. The loser ends up buying the winner's favorite piece among the five stores on our list."

"An expensive bet," Katherine said. "How are you holding up?"

"Not so good," Andrew frowned, running his fingers through his hair. "This is store #3 and she's two up on me. If I don't win here, I might as well concede.

"Can you give me the inside scoop? What are the best deals – and what are your favorite pieces? You must have exquisite taste."

Katherine's smile widened. "I think I can win you your bet, Mr.???"

"Call me Romeo," he winked.

Katherine giggled and then said in a hushed tone, "This way, please. The best items are over here."

Abby looked up in time to see Katherine walking Andrew to a display on the far side of the shop. To her relief, the other clerks were busily helping customers, and no one had approached her yet. The counter door was within her reach.

Suddenly, from outside the shop, a man's voice shouted loudly, "Thief! Thief! Somebody help!"

People craned their necks to see and seemed to start talking all at once. It was now or never.

Abby slid behind the counter and ducked into the back room, which had one door leading directly outback. There were no windows.

The room was dark and full of boxes. A bulky wooden table was off to the corner, and two other tables were next to a credenza.

Abby didn't know where to start or even what she was looking for. She had just started rummaging through some of the boxes when she heard footsteps approaching.

Quickly, she dove under the table and curled up as tightly as she could, hardly daring to breathe.

"What was all that about a thief?" a man's voice demanded. "We don't want any drama around here. Ralston is going to be here any minute."

"I don't know," the woman's voice stammered. "I think it must have been a false alarm – or it wasn't directed toward our store at least. The clerks just did a quick count, and nothing is missing."

"Well, I don't like it," the man said. "I'll feel better once Ralston moves his last boxful of the stuff. There's too much heat being generated around here. If they hadn't insisted we open our store front again, I'd have stayed closed for weeks."

"The story of a temporary rat infestation was brilliant," she said, trying to soften the conversation. "Besides, the authorities bought it; that's what matters."

"I don't like it. Anyway, when he gets here, give it to him, and let's close for the day. I need a drink."

"His suitcase is ready the minute he arrives, I assure you," she said. "Now, I need to get back to a customer."

The two left the room, and Abby uncurled herself to glance around the room, which remained dim and untouched.

Her mind raced as she thought on the words the woman had said, "His suitcase is ready." What suitcase?

Her eyes fell upon a leather duffle bag on top of the credenza. She reached for it and noticed a symbol imprinted on the leather. The symbol showed a cat's paw with claws extended. The last place she had seen that symbol was on the fanny pack she unearthed by

Susan's grave. That was moments before her assault in the cemetery.

Her pulse quickening, she unzipped the main compartment as quietly as she could. The moment she did so, a sickly sweet smell greeted her nostrils. It was the same smell she had noticed under Duff's back porch, moments before Neil had appeared.

Her fingers felt dozens of small squares, wrapped carefully in plastic. The smallest just fit inside the largest pocket of her shorts.

Her palms were sweating, and she knew time was against her. Ralston would be here soon enough. She zipped up the bag and returned it to its first position before cautiously moving toward the door.

It was locked, and as she fumbled to unlatch the deadbolt, a loud crash sounded from the shop followed by a child's wailing. It was all the invitation she needed to creak open the door and slip outside into the light.

Walking briskly, she hurried out of the alley until she reached one of the roads that would take her back to Bay Street. She hadn't seen anyone, but that didn't mean that no one had seen her.

"Hey, there you are!" a voice called from behind her, and she whirled around to see Freddy jogging to join her.

"Where were you?" Abby asked. "I didn't see you anywhere, so I thought I'd try to find my way to the Straw Market on my own."

"I was watching for you – or for anyone else. You had just disappeared around the corner when I saw a man start to make his way down the alley. I had to wait for him to enter the back door before running after you.

"That was close," Freddy heaved a sigh of relief. "But Mom's going to be really mad if we're late."

"Then let's hurry," Abby said. "I want to make sure the guys did okay out front."

"Did you find anything?" Freddy asked.

"I can't talk and run at the same time," Abby gasped. Their close getaway had left her knees wobbly, and she knew her breath capacity was no match for Freddy's incessant questions.

They reached the entrance to the makeshift Straw Market as the vendors were closing up for the day.

"Do you see them?" Abby asked, her eyes searching the myriad of tourists and Bahamians.

"No, but we'd better go find my mom. We're late, and she's not going to be happy about it."

"I have to find them," Abby said. "They don't even know how to reach me."

"I'm not letting you out of my sight," Freddy said firmly. "Coby will kill me when he finds out about this."

"He'll have to kill me first," Abby said. "Tell him I was too headstrong and you couldn't handle me."

"I'd rather he kill me than own up to that," Freddy grinned. He spotted his mom's truck several yards away, but she was not there.

"She may need help locking up her wares for the night. Come on – we'll look for your friends later."

Abby followed, not wanting to get Freddy into any more trouble. Mrs. Ward was just closing up for the day and did not seem to have noticed that they were tardy. For once, Abby appreciated the "grace" that Bahamian time could afford.

As they emerged from her venue, Abby caught sight of Steven, who was just out of earshot.

"Be back in a second," she whispered to Freddy and took off running. She could hear Mrs. Ward's exclamation of surprise.

"Steve!" she called.

"There you are," he sighed in relief, reaching to embrace her. "Andrew and I thought you were a goner."

"Are you both okay?" Abby asked.

"We're fine. The shop closed, and we didn't know if you had gotten out or not. Andrew's meeting up with the rest of our group, and I came here to check on you. What happened?"

Abby heard a horn honk behind her and knew she was trying Mrs. Ward's patience.

"Give me the number of wherever you're staying, and I'll call you tonight. I promise."

"I'm using my cell – It's a new number. Call me on that," Steven said, scribbling the number onto a receipt. "I'm worried about you, Abby."

"I'll call. I promise," Abby said and turned to leave. "Give Andrew my thanks – and tell him he's a better flirt than he'll ever care to admit."

The honking resumed, and Abby hurried back to the waiting truck. She was greeted by a hot, tired Mrs. Ward who was in no mood for antics.

"Miss Abby, what is the meaning of this?" she asked.

"That was my brother Steve," Abby said, slipping next to Freddy on the front seat. "I was so surprised to see him."

"Humph," she said and started down the road. Abby softened the conversation by asking about her day and her sales, which was all the invitation Mrs. Ward needed to vent about stingy and rude tourists.

The ride seemed endless till they reached the Wards, but when they did, Abby jumped out of the truck, excused herself and hurried to the house. She nearly collided with Coby at the door.

"What's the rush?" he smiled.

"I have to talk to you," she said.

"Now? I'm on my way to check on the boys."

"Yes, now."

Coby raised an eyebrow but followed Abby into the living room. Mrs. Ward had drafted Freddy to help her unload her truck, so for the moment, he could not interrupt.

"Now what's this all about?"

Abby did not reply but gently pulled a square-shaped object, bound tightly with layers of plastic, from her pocket. She handed it to Coby.

"I believe this is the evidence you've been looking for."

Coby gingerly unwrapped it to reveal a block of a flaky gray substance that smelled faintly sweet.

"Is this what I think it is?"

"I'm nearly certain it's the same thing I found at Duff's and at the graveside."

"Where did you get this?"

"At the same storefront that was closed two days ago but has reopened overnight," Abby said. "Apparently, the rat infestation is no longer a problem."

"Rat infestation?"

Abby started her story from the beginning, and by the time she finished, Coby was speechless.

"Have you told Rick yet?"

"I texted him to let him know I need to talk to him ASAP," Abby replied. "The fact that they are transporting this stuff in a duffle bag leads me to believe that Ralston would be making a trip with it. And I don't think he's going to Little Abaco."

"You think Rick's following a rabbit's trail?" Coby asked.

Abby nodded. "I think they wanted to get us off their scent and baited us with a false lead. We were so desperate for any news that we jumped at it. El GATO no longer viewed us as a threat, so they resumed operations.

"Or, they had laid plans so that no matter what we did, we would no longer be a threat. I think Rick needs to keep his eyes open for a trap."

Coby chuckled. "You sound like you have this figured out."

"Not everything. I don't know where they are planning to take the shipment or where they want to rendezvous with their clients. And those are big gaps to our puzzle."

"Well, I'm going to do two things right now," Coby said. "I'm going to put this in a safe place and send a sample to the lab. I want you to call Rick. We'll regroup in half an hour."

Abby nodded and hurried up to her room. She kicked off her shoes, flipped open her laptop, and pulled her phone out of her pocket. There were two missed calls from Rick.

She pressed the redial key and waited. He picked up on the second ring, and she retold her story.

Abby finally paused for breath and waited for Rick's response. Never before had she heard him this angry.

"Abby, that has to be the most insane trick you've pulled this whole trip. Think about what may have happened if you had been caught. Think about who saw you. Think about what they're going to do when they find out you took a sample. Just think about that."

"Well, you're very welcome," Abby retorted. "And besides, you would have done the same thing."

"That's beside the point. You're not a professional, and you don't even begin to understand the ramifications."

"Try me," Abby said. "First, this means you're on a wild goose chase in Little Abaco when the real action is happening somewhere else. It means El GATO no longer perceives us as a threat or has already given someone specific instructions to silence us. It also means time isn't on our side. If this is the last shipment, the deal is closing soon – even sooner than Wednesday."

"Not bad for a beginner, but you're forgetting one key detail," Rick said. "No one but us knew we were going to investigate the shop Saturday morning. Our own intelligence provided the Little Abaco tip.

"And if you want to go farther back, how were we so quickly detected on Paradise Island? Why was El GATO so confident of our whereabouts that they attempted your blatant abduction only hours after we landed?"

"Their intelligence is really good?" Abby asked.

"It's good all right," Rick laughed scornfully. "Don't you get it? There's an insider who's feeding them our every move, and we're playing into their hands like pawns on a chess board."

Abby was speechless.

"The question is who," Rick continued. "Owens was the one who communicated the Little Abaco tip."

"But Owens seems so nice," Abby countered.

"Good looks can be deceiving," Rick said.

"What about the Wards?"

"I trust them with my life," Rick said.

"Money does strange things to people," Abby said.

Rick sighed. "My gut says it's impossible, but if the Wards are behind this, you just gave them all our evidence, and there's no one to protect you."

Abby gulped. "Who else could it be?"

"The immediate people involved in the case are myself, you, the Wards, Brightly and Owens. Still, there are a number of other people related to the case that you don't even know about."

"When will you be coming back here?" Abby asked.

"Soonest flight I can get," Rick said. "In the meantime, you move from the Ward's property, I ground you for life."

"Whatever you say, Uncle, but I really don't think anyone detected me."

"You just remember that your success today is nothing short of miraculous."

"I thought I'd never hear you say those words," Abby said.

"Pure luck is what I meant. Babies don't ever cry at the right times, and diversions never go as planned."

"But mine weren't planned," Abby said. "They were Providence."

"This has nothing to do with God," Rick snapped. "If God were behind this, he would have hog-tied you to your bedpost and never let you leave your room today."

"You just don't believe in him," Abby said.

"No, I don't. You don't know the number of times I could have used his help, and he never came through. Trust me; I tried prayer when your Aunt Jane lay dying of cancer."

"Aunt Jane believed," Abby said.

"A bunch of good it did her."

"God sometimes doesn't answer prayer like we want him to," Abby said.

"Same principle with luck," Rick retorted. "Sometimes it wears thin, sometimes it doesn't. But at least it never promises to always be with you, like your loving God. And he comes up short half the time anyway."

"But Rick. . ."

"Don't get me started," he cut her off sharply. "You just do what I say from now on. I'm going on the premise I can still trust Coby, and I'll be back to Nassau by tomorrow morning. You do whatever he tells you, and he will tell you to stay put. No more adventures with your brother and friend."

"What about my report for tonight?" Abby asked.

"Don't send it. I don't know who I can trust anymore."

After final instructions, Abby hung up and sighed. She knew it was time for dinner and that Mrs. Ward would send Freddy to fetch her soon.

First, she remembered her promise to Steven and dialed the number he had given her. She was disappointed to have to leave a message. She wanted to hear his side of the story – details about the diversion and how Andrew managed to distract Katherine.

But it would have to wait. Besides, it would all be over soon enough. Either Rick would crack the case and they'd get to return heroes, or she would be poisoned by conch salad tonight and die ignorant.

The thought of conch salad alone made her stomach churn, and her overactive imagination suggesting it could be poisoned didn't help. But Freddy had insisted it was a delicacy and that she would have to try it at supper.

With a wry smile, Abby wondered if poison weren't a happier alternative.

— — — — — — — — — — — — —

Daylight was dwindling, and it was the time of evening when the bars along Bay Street were filling up, and the shops, locking down. The sign outside South American Treasures read closed, and to any observer, the establishment appeared empty.

But inside the barred windows, beyond the shop counter, a faint glow could be detected. A group of three – one man and two women – were huddled around the wooden table. The man was the owner of the establishment. He was smoking a thick cigar and thumping his fingers along the table's edge. His eyes were bloodshot and twitched nervously. The first woman was the shop clerk Katherine, and the second, an American woman, dressed efficiently in a trim navy suit.

The three sat in silence, reviewing the day's surveillance video on a small screen.

"There," the American spoke at last, pausing the video. "A young woman just slipped behind the counter.

"Impossible," the man sputtered. "My clerks would never let someone past the counter."

"See for yourself," the woman said dryly.

"Well, Katherine, how could this happen?"

"There were two distractions today," she faltered. "Someone called a false alarm about a thief, and then there was the child who broke the vase. It's possible that no one was at the counter . . ."

"You fool, that is the definition of diversion," the woman said. "I told you that you must be extremely careful."

"That was before the shop closed," the owner defended himself. "You were the one who told us it was safe to reopen the store front. I didn't want to, but you insisted. Oh my nerves!"

"Shut up," the woman said, unpausing the video. They watched the rest of it, but no one reemerged from the back room.

"She must have exited out the back," she said, rewinding the video. She replayed the section that showed the woman slipping behind the counter.

"It's impossible to see her face," the man cried. "We don't even know who she is."

"Wait, I recognize her shirt," Katherine said. "It's a sky blue color. I was helping her fiancé with some jewelry."

"Did you get a look at her face?" demanded the owner.

"No, I didn't. She was examining one of our displays."

The American was silent, her eyes intent on the video. Suddenly, she paused it again and caught a glimpse of the young woman's profile.

"Ah, so we are getting somewhere!" the owner sighed in relief. But the American woman suddenly stiffened.

"I think I've seen her in the store before," Katherine said, "but it was several days ago."

"I know who she is."

Both the owner and Katherine turned to face their American accomplice.

"And who would that be, Ms. Brightly?"

Edith's face relaxed. "It's of no importance. You won't be seeing her again."

"Well, I should think that you would tell me. After all, this is . . ." the owner began, but Edith cut him off.

"Thank you for your time," she said, picking up her handbag and rising from her seat. She pulled out a check and handed it to the owner. "Here is the agreed payment. We'll be in touch."

And with that, she walked out the back door and headed to where her jeep was parked. After starting the engine, she reached for her cell phone and hit speed dial.

"Neil, it's Edith. It appears Benton knows more than we thought."

"What do you mean?"

"His partner has been snooping around the shop. She managed to get behind the counter."

"You mean Abby?"

"Who else?" Edith snapped.

"I can't believe it."

"I've seen the video surveillance, and it's her, no doubt."

"Did she find anything?"

"I don't know. Nothing was disturbed – unless she discovered the suitcase."

"You mean the duffle bag Ralston delivered?"

"Yes. Have you had a chance to inspect it?"

"No, Ralston just arrived half an hour ago."

"Whether she found the bag or not is irrelevant," Edith said. "Whatever she knows is too much. Also, I've heard from our man on Little Abaco. Benton has purchased a ticket and is planning to fly back to Nassau tomorrow morning."

"Thank you, Brightly. Wait for your orders. I'll be in touch within the hour," Neil said and hung up.

He was seated on a bar stool in his employer's private lounge. On one side of the room was the self-serve bar and on the other side, a large sitting area that opened up into a long balcony. The sun had since disappeared, but the sound of waves breaking on the sand was clearly audible. A man with frosted hair, broad shoulders and a large build was standing with his back toward Neil, his face looking out into the night. His perfectly pressed suit and flawless collection of first edition books lining the lounge bookshelves revealed his passion for detail; his impassive eyes and scarred, massive hands suggested his tendency toward cruelty. The man was Vladimir Zarchoff.

"Are the rumors about a breach at the shop confirmed?" he asked, puffing at his cigar.

"Yes, Sir, apparently from the surveillance video."

"And it was Benton's niece behind it?"

"If that's what you want to call Abigail Grant, then yes," Neil replied. "I'm not sure I buy the whole niece cover."

"You should do more research," Zarchoff replied. "She is most definitely his niece – and apparently, his partner as well."

"Speaking of Benton, our sources say he is flying to Nassau tomorrow morning," Neil continued.

Zarchoff was silent. Neil knew better than to interrupt his thoughts.

Finally, he spoke. "I think that a short trip for Miss Grant is in order. I will be delighted to meet her."

"You want me to bring her here? Even with Fedor and Mikhail flying in tomorrow? They're scheduled to arrive early in the afternoon to deliver the remaining payment and supervise the shipment."

"They'll never know she is here, and besides, I'm afraid she won't be with us for long. Just long enough to serve our purpose."

"Benton and Ward?"

"Precisely. How do the Americans say it? Killing two birds with one stone."

Chapter 14

A Bad Aftertaste

A bby woke early in the morning to an upset stomach. For fear of being rude, she had allowed Mrs. Ward to persuade her to seconds of conch chowder, and she was feeling the cruel aftermath.

She rummaged in her purse hoping to find an antacid tablet and with relief, located one. Then, she tossed herself back onto her bed and stared at the ceiling as she waited for her stomach to take command of itself again.

After several failed attempts at falling back asleep, she finally looked at her clock. It was 5:30 in the morning, and her unsatisfying night made her eager to get out of bed.

She tossed on a simple yellow sundress and sat down on the chair in her room, her toes toying with the sandals below her. With her stomach now settled, she longed to take a walk down the beach to watch the sunrise. But discretion won out, and she settled for a book instead.

Her eyelids were starting to feel heavy from reading, and with a yawn, she folded the book in her lap and let her eyes close.

It seemed like a dream when only minutes later, she felt a rough hand clamp around her mouth. Her eyes popped open, only to see a blur of a face in front of her.

She tried to jump out of the chair, but a damp cloth was being pressed against her eyes and nose. The room started to spin, and she felt herself try to resist whoever was grabbing her. Moments later, she lost consciousness and crumpled into the man's arms.

"Too easy, easier than the first time," Kurt muttered to himself. "I should've just hit you a little harder the last time around."

Into his phone, he said, "I've got her. Meet me around back."

Brightly replied, "Neil's already at the airport. Make it snappy."

Tossing Abby over his shoulder, Kurt pulled the note from his pocket, flung it on the bed, and silently slipped out around back. He passed the man he had clubbed when making his entry and paused just long enough to confirm he was still out. Then, he hurried to the neighboring lot, reached the black sedan, and placed the girl in the back.

"Let's go," he told Brightly, as he jumped into the passenger seat.

"Did you meet anyone?"

"Only the guard out front, but he wasn't a problem."

"How long will she be out for?"

"Probably an hour. That's long enough to get to the airport and be in mid-flight. I can administer more, but I wasn't sure if you or Neil wanted to talk with her."

"That's fine. I'm sure Neil will have some choice words."

"She still doesn't know about you, does she?"

"Not yet, but she will soon enough. Let's just say I'm the expert at interrogation. I'll soon know everything she knows – everything she should have reported to me in the e-mail she never sent."

They drove the rest of the way in silence. Upon reaching the airport, Brightly drove toward a private hangar where the small craft was waiting, nearly ready for take-off.

Kurt wrapped the still unconscious Abby in a black blanket to avoid detection. Once inside the craft, he laid her in the back row of seats and joined Brightly and DeWitt up front.

"Everything is going like clockwork," Neil said. "We'll land just after 7:00 o'clock. Benton's flight isn't scheduled to arrive until two hours later. We'll already be to Cat Island by the time he knows she's missing.

"Brightly, there is one slight change. I want you to be in Nassau when Benton arrives, to make sure everything goes as planned."

"Benton doesn't suspect anything, I'm sure of that," Brightly said. "Don't you want me to stay with the girl? I told you I'd make her talk."

"Thank you for the offer, Edith, but I'm quite capable of handling the girl. I want you to keep tabs on Benton. He may see right through our little game. I want you to make sure he and Ward follow the scent to Cat Island. Zarchoff made clear that he wants to wrap up several things today: the deal with the Russians – and his unsatisfying relationship with those two investigators."

"If I discover he isn't following the plan, I'll make myself known to him. I'll tell him I'm joining him in Nassau at Agent Owens' order and that we are concerned with the lack of communication from him over the last two days," Edith replied coolly.

"Fine. We'll see you later today," Neil said. Into the cockpit he yelled, "Captain, let's get this bird off the ground."

"If you don't mind, I'm going to grab some shut eye," Kurt said, fastening his seat belt for take off.

"Is kidnapping unsuspecting females too exhausting for you?" Neil smirked.

"Hardly," Kurt laughed. "But I've been up all night planning with Brightly and casing the Ward's home. Besides, I think you and the kid can use a heart to heart, and I'd hate to interrupt."

"Sweet dreams," Neil joshed.

Kurt snorted but did not reply.

The plane started to taxi down the runway as Neil walked back to where Abby lay in a heap on the seat.

He could see just the top of her head. He pulled back the blanket far enough to see her face.

He saw for a moment the little girl who had tossed punch onto his shirt. He saw for a moment the young woman in pink pajamas who met him with suspicion at the door, the one who insisted on being a light sleeper. He remembered her look of surprise when she uncovered the stowed package under the porch.

The black blanket slipped to reveal the sleeve of her yellow sundress.

Black and yellow – It was the color of sunflowers. Why did she always remind him of his sister?

He turned to look out the window. He told himself the girl beside him was a sleuth trying to destroy everything he had worked so hard for. He told himself that when she opened her eyes, he would take no pity. He would do his job. He would make a success of himself, regardless of who he had to trample.

His sister was dead. If Abigail happened to look like a sunflower, it was of no consequence to him. Beauty no longer belonged in his world.

— — — — — — — — — — — — — — —

Freddy awoke Tuesday morning to the sound of excited voices coming from the kitchen. He tossed his covers aside, slipped a shirt over his head, and hurried out of his room to discover the cause for all the noise.

The first sight that met him was his brother AJ, seated in a chair, and trying to keep his mother from fussing over a large gouge in his forehead.

Coby was talking to Jacob and Warren as they appeared to examine a piece of paper centered on the kitchen table.

"What's going on?" Freddy asked. No one bothered to answer, for they were all absorbed in conversation.

Freddy frowned and helped himself to an empty seat around the table. He looked uneasily at his brothers, who did not seem to have noticed that he had entered the room.

He repeated his first question and finally got Warren's attention.

"AJ was watching the grounds this morning, and someone clubbed him," Warren replied.

"You okay?" Freddy turned to AJ.

"Fine, if our Straw Lady would stop all this fussing," he complained.

"Did you catch the person? Where's Abby?"

The room was silent for a minute, and Coby finally turned to his youngest brother.

"Look, Freddy, Abby's been kidnapped."

For a brief moment, Freddy was speechless. He looked from one brother to the next as the reality settled. Coby handed him a piece of paper, and he read:

Rendezvous at New Bight no later than 10:00 a.m. Bring brick of cargo in exchange for Grant. Come alone, and ask for Charlie. First and Last Chance.

Freddy read and re-read the short note. "But who? Why?"

Coby took the note from him and replied, "It's got the makings of El GATO all over it. They've taken her to Cat Island. That's either a cruel play on words, or they actually have some kind of operations located there. Either way, that's where they've taken Abby."

"Sure, I get the New Bight part, but where do we go from there? We don't have much time to look if we have to meet them by 10 o'clock," Freddy protested.

"Oh, they told us where to find them," Coby replied. "First and Last Chance is a small bar outside the airport before you reach New Bight. It's an established venue, and they want us to meet them there."

"But the note says, 'Come alone.' Does that mean Mr. Benton?"

"Of course it means Rick," Coby said, setting his jaw. "But I wouldn't send a friend of mine in alone. Not when I know El GATO's history so well. They'll never do a fair exchange."

"But we've got to save Abby," Freddy persisted. "We've got to do something."

"Freddy, this is Rick's and my case, and we'll do what we can."

"I want to help," Freddy insisted.

"You can help – by staying put. You need to watch the house and help your brothers. Whoever took Abby knows where we live, and our home is no longer a safe place. I need you to do whatever you can to help keep your family safe here."

Freddy knew better than to protest. He knew Coby didn't want him getting in the way. But he also didn't think Coby understood that he was a man too and could be of more help in the center of the action – instead of at home with his mom.

"I'm going to pick up Rick at the airport, and we'll go from there. Jacob, I'll keep you updated. You have Rick's contacts back at the office, and I've already informed them of the situation."

After Coby had left, Mrs. Ward stopped her fussing and regained her composure. As she bustled about to make breakfast, Freddy slipped upstairs to Abby's room.

The bed was haphazardly made, and he could only detect slight signs of a struggle. Walking over to the chair, he bent down to pick up a book strewn on the floor. It was one of Abby's Agatha Christie books. Beside it was a receipt she must have been using for a bookmark.

He turned it over to see a phone number, and then he remembered where he had seen it before. It was the number her brother had handed to her yesterday before she had hurried to meet his mom and him at the truck.

His mother's voice was calling him, so he slipped the paper in his pocket and hurried down the stairs.

"Freddy, stop daydreaming, and eat your breakfast," she said, wiping her hands on her apron. "I have to be to work in an hour. Your brothers may need the truck today, so I want you to take me to work and then come right home. You understand?"

"Yes, Ma'am," Freddy replied, sliding into his chair at the table. His hand felt for his pocket and the piece of paper.

To a fifteen-year-old boy, understanding and obeying are not necessarily the same thing.

— — — — — — — — — — — — — — —

Andrew awoke to the sound of a cell phone ringing. He, Matt and friends had stayed up late last night. After dinner, they returned to the Browns' place to talk about the new church and upcoming ceremony.

He couldn't remember the last time he had seen Matt and Jimmy so happy to be seeing the results of their ministry. Field time was just what they needed – Ian couldn't have been more right about that.

But there was something else too, and Andrew's instincts told him it had something to do with Kim and Amber. Matt was quite devoted to Amber, and for the first time, Andrew noticed Jimmy paying attention to Kim. They had been short a menu at dinner, so Jimmy shared his with Kim. They just happened to sit next to each other at the table and happened to fall behind everyone else as the group walked along Bay Street.

He and Steven, on the other hand, hadn't enjoyed the evening half as much. It seemed every fifteen minutes, Steven was checking his cell phone, and every other five minutes, he was asking Steven if he had checked it. The two had downplayed to the group their meeting with Abby, because neither really understood the dynamics of the situation.

But both agreed something was wrong, and until they had assurances that Abby was fine, neither could take full advantage of the relaxing evening.

And then, Steven had missed her when she did call, because they were saying goodnight to the Browns and girls.

Since the ceremony didn't start until 10 a.m., the four had decided to sleep in until 8:00 o'clock, grab a quick breakfast, and then get to the groundbreaking location early to help with any set up.

So when Andrew heard a phone ringing at 7:30, he reached for his, but it was off. He looked at Steven, who was rummaging to find his own.

"Hello?" Steven asked.

"Hi, you don't know me, but are you Abby's friends?"

"Yes, who is this?"

"My name's Freddy Ward, and she was staying at my house until she was kidnapped this morning."

"She was what?" Steven shouted, forgetting that Matt and Jimmy were still asleep. Heads sprang up from around the room, and there was no use apologizing.

"Look, I'm not good at this talking on a phone and driving at the same time thing. Where can I meet you?"

"Is this some kind of blackmail?" Steven demanded.

"You got the wrong idea, Mister," Freddy retorted. "I'm trying to figure out how to save her, and I thought you might like to help."

"Okay, okay, where can we meet you?" Steven scribbled down the directions, assured the boy they'd be there, and hung up.

"Who was that, or don't I want to know?" Andrew asked.

"It's the kid we saw with Abby yesterday," he replied, already getting dressed. "I don't know exactly what's happened, but he says Abby's been kidnapped, and he wants to save her."

Andrew didn't reply but jumped off the couch and threw open his suitcase.

"What's going on?" Matt yawned from under his sheets.

"It may be a prank, or it may be real, but we got a call about Abby being in some kind of trouble," Steven replied. "I'm going to meet the caller in ten minutes close to the Straw Market."

"And I'm going with him," Andrew said, trying to find his other shoe.

"We'll all go," Jimmy said.

"No, you two stay here. This may be nothing. Either way, we'll call you, but I'd hate to see all of us late – or miss – the ceremony this morning since that's what we came for," Steven said.

"You promise to call us the minute you know," Jimmy said.

"Will do," Andrew replied, following Steven out the door.

They flagged a taxi and said nothing during the duration of the ride. Both were thinking that they would be seriously upset with this teenager if this were some sort of prank – and yet, at the same time, they hoped it was nothing more than a simple prank.

Steven spotted the pickup truck he had seen Abby enter yesterday evening parked in some grass. He paid the taxi, and the two approached the vehicle. The Bahamian boy appeared, clad in plaid shorts and a t-shirt a size too big.

Andrew recognized him as Freddy.

"Look, what's going on here?" Andrew demanded.

Freddy ignored him and turned to Steven. "It's just like I told you. Abby's been kidnapped. If you don't believe me, read this. I managed to grab it when my brothers weren't looking."

Steven read the note, eyes furrowed.

"First and Last Chance is a bar on Cat Island," Freddy explained before Steven had a chance to ask. "That's obviously where they've taken Abby."

"Or where they want us to think they've taken her," he said. "Who do they mean when they say, 'Come alone'?"

"They mean Rick Benton, of course," Freddy said.

"And what is Rick doing about this note?" Steven asked.

"I don't know yet. He is flying in to Nassau this morning. But if he treats this note like he treated the situation last Friday when we thought Abby had been abducted on Paradise Island …"

"What?" Andrew interrupted. "You mean this isn't the first attempt?"

"No, it's not. And last time, Rick didn't do a thing," Freddy retorted. "I'm not going to stand around and wait. I'm going to do something about it."

"And that's why you called us?" Steven asked.

Freddy hesitated. "I figured you would want to help, Abby being your sister and all. That's why I called you."

"So what exactly is your plan?" Andrew asked.

"I suggest we catch a plane and go to Cat Island ourselves and rescue her."

Andrew whistled. "Just like that."

Freddy frowned at him. Before he could argue, Steven said, "Look, Freddy, of course we want to help. But I think we need to be realistic here. Andrew and I don't know anything about this case, except for that crazy idea of Abby's for sneaking inside a jewelry store.

"Like it or not, we have to work with Rick on this."

"What if he doesn't do anything?" Freddy said.

Andrew and Steven looked at each other. "We'll make sure he does."

— — — — — — — — — — — — — — — —

Never in his life had Rick felt so out of control.

He had rushed back as soon as he could, and El GATO had still beaten him to his niece. His stomach tightened as Coby told him of the ransom note, but he wasn't surprised. Tomorrow was the rumored delivery deadline, and he knew El GATO would stop at nothing to make sure they closed the deal on time – if not early.

No sooner did they arrive at Coby's place than the Ward's familiar pick-up truck pulled into the driveway, bringing a frustrated Freddy and his passengers.

Rick was stunned to see Steven and Andrew. After brief introductions, he asked, "What are you two doing here?"

"It's a long story," Andrew said. "It started when Freddy …"

The story tumbled out, with Freddy interrupting every few minutes.

"We just want to get Abby back," Steven said, "and we'll do anything we can to help."

"Then you'd better leave it to me," Rick said, turning away from them.

"You did nothing when Abby was missing on Paradise Island," Freddy blurted out.

"Freddy!" Coby said.

Rick was about to reply when his cell phone rang. He looked at the caller ID and without a word, walked out of the room. No one said anything for the next few minutes. Finally, Rick returned.

"That was Brightly," he said to Coby. "She is on her way to Nassau."

"I called the office when we received the note," Coby explained. "I had to leave a message for Owens to let him know about Abby."

"She said that Owens received a tip just this morning that the Russian deal is going down at Cat Island this afternoon. She's arranged a plane for us. We are to accompany her to Cat Island."

Coby frowned. "And what? Just like that we're going to waltz into Last Chance Bar and exchange the missing brick for Abby?"

"She said we are to make the exchange and then follow through on the tip. She said there is a private, secluded estate where they anticipate the deal to take place."

"It sounds a little too simple to me."

"It's simple all right," Rick snapped. "It's simply a trap."

"Do you trust Brightly?"

"No, I don't trust Brightly. I don't know who to trust anymore," he muttered.

Coby looked at him. "Rick, I don't know who is against you, but I am for you. I'll do whatever I can to help you find Abby."

"El GATO is using Abby as bait," Rick said. "Can't you see? We'll never get past Last Chance Bar to investigate this so-called tip. We'll play right into their hands and never have a chance to stop the shipment."

Before Coby could reply, Steven cut in. "Excuse me, but what's more important to you? Solving this case or saving my sister?"

"Steven's right," Andrew said. "Trap or no trap, where's your heart? This is your niece we're talking about."

Rick turned away and closed his eyes. He saw his niece, sitting next to him in the car, filled with excitement over the camera he had just handed her. She looked so innocent in her tank top and Bermuda shorts. He remembered Coby ribbing him that his brothers wouldn't leave her alone when they discovered his little niece was an attractive young woman. He thought back to his last conversation with her. Her words still rang in his ears, "God sometimes doesn't answer prayer like we want him to …"

"Rick?" It was Coby's deep voice, filled with concern.

"You're right," Rick finally said. "This isn't about me. This is about Abby. Whatever it takes to get her back, that's what we're going to do."

"What do you have in mind? Brightly will be here in under an hour," Coby guessed, looking at his watch.

"Whatever your plan is, we want to help," Steven said.

"I don't think that's a great idea," Rick started, but Andrew cut him off. "Look, Rick, we already know it's not a good situation. You just as much said you don't know who you can trust. Well, you can trust us."

Coby nodded. "They do have a point. If Brightly and Owens are in league with El GATO, we could use a few good men."

Rick sighed. "All right."

"It's settled then," Steven said, pulling out his cell phone. To Andrew, he said, "I'm going to call Jimmy and let him know what's going on."

"Brightly doesn't know about these two," Coby thought out loud. "What if they pretend to be some extra passengers on the flight to Cat Island? Maybe they could get a head start and arrive at the bar before you – or El GATO – gets there."

"And what about you?" Rick asked his friend.

"I'm not going to let the two of us get caught in the same place," Coby replied. "There would be nothing more satisfying to our enemies than for us to go down together. I think I'll look into this 'tip' from Brightly while you make the exchange for Abby. I know some people on the island who can help me find out what the inside story is.

"In the meantime, I'm going to call in reservations for two more tickets to Cat Island," Coby said, leaving the room.

"My cell phone is dead," Steven muttered. "I left it on all night, waiting for Abby to call."

Andrew felt for his own phone in his pocket and let out a groan. "I must have left mine at the hotel. We'd better hurry back to tell Jimmy and Matt what's going on."

"There isn't time," Rick said. "You're going to need to leave for the airport in fifteen minutes. I'll help you get some stuff together if you want to use the phone here."

"Thanks, but that won't help," Steven sighed. "I don't have Matt's or Jimmy's numbers memorized, and we discovered last night that the phone in our hotel room isn't working."

"What about me?" Freddy interrupted.

Rick grinned. "These guys are going to need a chauffer to the airport. You're our man."

"But I want to go too," he protested.

Rick grew solemn. "Freddy, this isn't a game. If this trap is as well-laid as I suspect, it will be nothing short of miraculous if all four of us come back tonight."

"Abby believes in God," Freddy said. "She would tell you nothing is impossible with him."

"So she's gotten you to believe her wishful thinking too," Rick scoffed.

"I don't buy it all," Freddy retorted. "I just think that if she has so much faith in him, it might not be a bad idea to try to a have a little hope too."

— — — — — — — — — — — — — —

"Now faith is the substance of things hoped for, the evidence of things not seen."

Pastor Brown's booming voice spread through the open-air gathering and pulled Jimmy's thoughts back to the present. He just couldn't keep his mind from wandering. Where were Steven and Andrew? Were they on their way? What was going on with Abby?

He glanced at Kim next to him, and she seemed intent upon the speaker's words for this ground-breaking ceremony.

His gaze swept past her to the crowd gathered together. All eyes were fastened upon Edward Brown, whose sermon was giving them the encouragement to press on with their church building and church family.

But Jimmy just couldn't concentrate. He felt his phone in his pocket, which he had reluctantly silenced for the service. Maybe he had missed Steven's call. Maybe Steven needed to talk to him.

He could bear it no longer. He stepped away and headed toward the back of the gathering, the pastor's voice still audible behind him.

"But without faith, it is impossible to please him."

Impatiently, he waited for his phone to show a signal. Finally, he dialed voicemail and listened.

"There are no new messages in your voice mailbox," the voice recording said.

He flipped his phone shut in frustration. Where were those two? Surely they would have called by now. They had promised they would call.

Some twigs snapped behind him, and he turned to see Kim, just feet away. She smiled awkwardly. "I wondered where you were going."

Jimmy sighed, "I just needed to check my phone."

Her eyes spoke her concern. "I'm sorry, Jimmy. I'm sure they're all right."

"How can you be sure? Steven's last words to me keep playing over and over in my mind – like I'm having a bad dream. What could have happened to Abby? And who would have even known where to find us to tell us?"

He stuffed the phone back in his pocket and looked toward the sky. A moment later, he felt a hand softly slip into his.

233

"I'm sorry, Jimmy. I don't know that everything's all right. But God knows. And I know he cares very much for your brother and sister and Andrew."

He squeezed her hand back. "You're right, Kim. Let's go back to the meeting."

"Do you want to pray first?"

He looked down at the young woman beside him. "Would you?"

She nodded. "God, I know you're there, and I thank you that you hear our prayers. Please protect Steve and Andrew and Abby. We don't know what has happened, but you do. We feel helpless, but we know you are strong. Help us to trust you, for you have said that you will renew the strength of those who wait upon you, that you will help them to mount up with eagles' wings, that you will make them walk without weariness and run without fainting."

"Amen," Jimmy said.

Chapter 15

First and Last Chance

A low droning noise first awakened her senses. At first, it sounded like humming and then more like a neighbor mowing his lawn. But surely it was too early to be mowing.

Abby blinked her eyes and felt the stuffy air trapped between a fuzzy blanket and her face. Slowly, her fingers peeled back the cover, and a rush of light made her eyes ache. She squinted and pulled the blanket back over her face.

Where was she? The humming noise was starting to sound like the muffled roar of a plane's engine. Her body began to sense the movement that comes from riding in a plane.

Her mind slowly started to patch together a memory. She had wanted to walk on the beach, but she hadn't. She had been too awake to go back to bed. Hadn't she started to read? There seemed to have been a bad dream where she was struggling with someone, but surely it had just been a dream.

Voices from the front of the plane reached her ears, and she cautiously pulled the blanket back from her face. Above her was a bright white ceiling with storage compartments lining the oval interior.

Directly beside her was the back of three seats through the cracks of which she could discern a man's figure, slumped in a seat several rows ahead of her. She forced her eyes to focus.

"Kurt," she thought to herself, revolting against the very thought of what must have happened.

She had been kidnapped.

Her mind starting spinning, and she remembered what Rick had told her before, about what would happen if she were abducted. Her first reaction was fear, which starting pricking her thoughts with questions about where she was being taken and what they were going to do with her.

She wasn't a trained spy. She didn't know the first thing about how to respond to interrogation.

"Stop it, Abby," she scolded herself. "You're working yourself up. Think about what is true."

She closed her eyes and concentrated by thinking about the mission, about that small office where she had stuffed envelopes for hours. What she wouldn't give right now to be back there.

She thought about Andrew. Why hadn't she listened to him? Why had she been headstrong? Surely it was her own fault she was in this fix.

"God, I'm so sorry," she whispered. "I thought I had to have this job, to do things in my own strength, in my own way. I know you allow everything for a purpose, though. Please work this out for good ... somehow."

She kept her eyes closed and tried to remember her favorite Bible verse. The words of Psalm 139 came back like a soothing balm. "If I take the wings of the morning, and dwell in the uttermost parts of the sea; Even there shall thy hand lead me, and thy right hand shall hold me."

The words played over again in her thoughts, and in combination with the lingering effects of chloroform, returned her to a temporary slumber.

When she blinked open her eyes fifteen minutes later, her senses had sharpened, and the feeling of panic had died away.

But in its place remained the fear of the unknown and a sense of urgency for the situation. Today was Tuesday, the day before the shipment was rumored to change hands. As much as Abby may have wanted to hide under the blanket, she knew she had to find answers.

As she started to rise from her reclined position, she suddenly froze when she realized a man was sitting directly in front of her.

It was Neil. He turned to face her. "Our sleeping beauty has awakened."

Abby sat up straight and returned his stare. For a moment, neither said anything.

"You know, when I saw you at Duff's place, I thought you were rather harmless," Neil finally said. "I thought you were as scatterbrained as my cousin and just another nosy kid. But now it all makes sense. You were a plant, a spy. I don't know how the DEA detected me, but they made a smart choice in choosing you – until now."

Abby did not respond but turned to look out the window to watch as the plane passed mile upon mile of crystal blue water.

"I do hope you'll be a smart girl and cooperate."

Still looking out the window, she replied, "I don't understand how the Bahamas can be so deceptively beautiful."

Finally, she turned to face him. Neil simply stared at her, clearly not having anticipated her response.

She continued, "Last night, I looked out from my balcony onto a pristine beach to watch the sun set. And now, I find myself on a plane to who knows where for a reason I cannot understand having a conversation with my friend's cousin."

"You know why you're here," Neil accused her.

"Because I'm Rick Benton's niece?"

"Because you're a spy."

"So that's what you think."

"That's what we know."

Abby turned away, and Neil frowned. He was getting nowhere with this approach.

"Tell me what you were doing in that shop."

Abby did not reply.

"You know perfectly well that I'm talking about the jewelry shop on Bay Street."

Abby's heart raced. Did Neil already know that she had been in the shop? Did he know what she had taken?

Neil watched her profile. Her lips were quivering, and she was fighting for composure. Either she was Benton's niece, and he had pulled her into this mix for cover; or she was a clever actress.

"Did Rick tell you to sneak into the shop? Did he tell you where to look for the shipment? There's no use in pretending. You can't argue with a surveillance tape. And we know one of the blocks was missing from the suitcase."

Abby took a deep breath. "Yes, I took it. Is that what you want to know?"

"What did you do with it?"

"I gave it to someone I trust."

Neil snorted. "Trust? Trust no one. Didn't your uncle teach you that? Well, my dear, let's hope for your sake that whoever you trusted so foolishly cares more about you than his career advancement."

A voice over the intercom interrupted their conversation. "We are now beginning our descent to Cat Island. Please fasten your seatbelts, and return your seats to an upright position as we prepare to land."

"Cat Island?" Abby said softly.

Neil smirked as he rose from his seat to return to the cockpit. "That's right. Fasten your seatbelt, Abby. You're in for a rough landing."

———————————————

When the small passenger flight landed at the New Bight airport on Cat Island, Andrew and Steven made it a point to be among the first off the craft.

239

Andrew had been stuffed between an overheated Bahamian man and a woman whose perfume was far too strong.

Steven had managed a more comfortable position next to a newly married couple, but Brightly and Ward had sat directly behind him. He had to listen to Brightly feed Coby "tips" about the location of the shipment.

"And what exactly is the Crow's Nest?" Coby had asked, trying not to sound suspicious.

"It's a secluded, privately owned estate northeast of the New Bight airport. Its remote location made it hard to detect," Brightly had whispered back.

The more he overheard Edith, the less Steven trusted her. Her neat little answers were equally as irritating to him as the overly strong perfume was to Andrew.

"Having to listen to that woman feed Coby information for a set-up is sickening," he gagged as the two looked for a taxi.

Andrew moaned. "True, but at least you haven't lost the sense of smell."

Steven grinned. "You'll recover. Come on, I think I see a taxi over there."

The two jogged over, but the cab was already full. They caught sight of another and were relieved to find it was available.

"Where to?" the Bahamian asked.

"First and Last Chance Bar," Steven replied.

"You don't want to stop at your hotel first?"

"No, we're meeting up with someone there," Andrew said.

"Is there room for one more?" a woman with a thick accent asked.

"Of course," the taxi man replied.

"It's her!" Andrew groaned. "I can smell her already."

"It's really important we get to the bar as soon as possible," Steven said to the man. "We're supposed to be meeting someone in ten minutes."

"No problem. I'll drop you boys off first and then take Madame …"

"My name is Verona Undine," the woman said, "and I'm staying at the Bridge Inn."

"No problem," the man replied, tipping his hat. "Hop on in."

Andrew coughed as the three-some piled in the cab. Steven cranked down the window, but the smell was still overwhelming.

After a few moments of silence, Andrew couldn't help himself. "That's a very um, powerful perfume you have."

"You like it? It used to be my husband's favorite. He would say it is quite unforgettable."

"I'd have to agree," Andrew muttered to himself.

"Why are we stopping?" she asked the driver. "This is not my hotel."

"These gentlemen are getting off here," he replied.

"Surely you could drop me off first!"

"Well, Ma'am, this small blue bar may not look like much, but the owner sells some of the finest straw work in the Bahamas. It's a great place to pick up a pint too, if you catch my drift."

"Fine straw work, you say," she said. "Well, wait here. I will go look myself."

Andrew and Steven had already paid the driver and hurried away.

"Unforgettable," Steven laughed, then grew serious. "Well, here we are. It's a pretty small place, and it looks like a harmless local spot."

"We could be on a wild goose chase," Andrew said.

"If not, whoever is supposed to meet Rick here certainly understands the element of surprise," Steven replied.

The two walked inside the small building. There were locals mulling about, playing dominoes and dousing beer. Some tourists were inspecting straw work, and others were reading or smoking at some of the tables.

"What do we do now?" Andrew whispered.

"I'm going to ask around for the best beaches to see if I can catch any conversations. You go check out the straw work."

"Straw work?"

"Unless you'd rather order a beer," Steven teased and walked over to where some local men were talking.

"Straw work," Andrew thought with a sigh and headed over to where some women were selling wares.

"Excuse me," he started lamely, "but I'm looking for something for my fiancé. What would you recommend?"

They smiled broadly. "What does your lady like?"

"What does she like?" he repeated. "Well, nothing too showy. Just something nice."

"What's her favorite color?"

"Um, blue," he replied, realizing he had no idea what Abby's favorite color was.

"Would she like a hat or purse better?"

"Actually, I was wondering if you might have seen her," he stammered. "You see, we were supposed to meet up here, but I think she may have headed back to our hotel."

"What does she look like?"

Andrew noticed out of the corner of his eye that an American man was intently studying him. The man was dressed in a loose, button down khaki shirt and had the makings of a beard. When Andrew looked his way, he resumed reading the paper.

"Is she tall or short?" the one woman asked, getting Andrew's attention.

"She's just right," he heard himself say, measuring to the top of his shoulder.

The ladies smiled at each other. "What a sweet thing to say. Well, there have only been two young women here this morning. The first one did some shopping and then left – that must have been your lady."

"What about the second?"

The two women looked at each other and frowned. "She came in with a rough crowd and didn't really say anything or do any shopping. The men with her just walked her to the bar and talked to the bar tender."

"She did ask for water, but the one man with her said she could wait until they got to the house," she sighed. "I felt sorry for her. It's such a shame when a young lovely little thing marries the wrong kind of man."

Andrew felt his heart start to race, but he managed to say, "Well then, I'm sure my fiancé was the first. Whatever you recommend, that's what I'll get."

At that moment, Rick walked in, carrying a small bag with him. He headed straight to the bar and ordered a beer before casting a glance around the small interior. It seemed like all eyes followed him.

"I'm looking for Charlie," he said to the bar tender but loud enough for everyone to hear.

Andrew caught Steven's eye and held his breath.

"He told me to tell you he's waiting for you around back," the man said, nodding toward a door behind him.

"No, I'd like for Charlie to meet me right here," Rick stated boldly.

Suddenly, the men who were playing dominoes flipped over their tables, causing their glasses to crash to the floor.

The women selling the straw products hurried out, not wanting to witness a fight. In doing so, they nearly collided with Verona Undine.

"Where can I find the fine straw products?" she asked.

As if her words were a signal, a brawl broke out. Men lunged for Rick, who was trapped at the bar.

"Andrew, over here!" Steven cried, throwing punches next to Rick.

Dropping the straw hat he was ready to buy, he hurled himself into the crowd, which was growing larger as men appeared from the back.

Rick seemed engulfed by Bahamian men, and Steven and Andrew ended up meeting by the door.

"This is crazy," Andrew muttered, swinging a chair to avoid a burly man's blow.

Steven was about to reply when a man's hand gripped his shoulder. "Follow me," the voice said, indicating the door.

Andrew and Steven didn't argue since it was pointless to try to reach Rick. When they had reached the parking lot, the man jumped into a jeep and turned on the engine.

"Get in!" he cried as several men emerged from the bar.

"Well?" Andrew asked.

"I'd rather take my chances with this character than those burly Bahamians," Steven said.

As the jeep drove away, Andrew had a chance to look at their unlikely friend. He recognized him as the man in the khaki shirt who had been watching him in the bar.

"Who are you?" Andrew asked.

"The question is: who are you?" he replied. "And what do you know about Rick Benton?"

"He happens to be my uncle," Steven said.

"You're Abigail's brother?"

"Twin brother, to be exact."

"And what exactly were you doing in that bar?"

"It's a long story," Steven said.

"And we still don't know who you are," Andrew added.

"The name's Garth Owens," he replied. "I'm with the DEA and working with Benton and his niece on this case."

"Do you by any chance work with someone by the name of Brightly?" Steven asked.

Owens looked at him sharply. "What do you know about her?"

"Nothing much, except that she met Rick and Coby Ward this morning with news of a tip on Cat Island. Rick seemed a little wary of the information."

Owens was silent for a moment. Then he said, "Why don't you start at the beginning of your story?"

"I don't mean to sound rude, but how do we know you're who you say you are?" Steven asked.

Owens smiled and pulled out his identification. "I didn't fly all the way from Washington DC to the Bahamas at 2 o'clock this morning for nothing. After losing contact with Rick and discovering that Brightly had been feeding me bad information, I decided I needed to come down here myself to find out what's going on."

Steven handed him back his ID and started with his story.

"Brightly said the shipment was changing hands at a place called the Crow's Nest, somewhere northeast of the New Bight airport," Steven concluded.

"Do you think that's where they've taken Abby?" Andrew asked.

"Could be," Owens said, "or it could be just another trap like the bar."

"What about Rick?" Steven asked.

Owens sighed and glanced at his phone. "I'm waiting to hear from my man who is following the abductors from a distance."

"Not to be all gloom and doom, but what do these people want from Rick and Abby?"

"Well, if Rick took with him the one bargaining chip in his possession, namely, a piece of the shipment, there's only one thing left that they could possibly want."

"And that is?"

"Revenge."

"For what?"

Owens paused. "This is all classified, but the heart of the matter is that the organization behind this case had a run in with Rick many years back. Rick's detective work cost them a lot of money."

Garth's phone chirped, and he answered. "Hullo?" There was a pause. "Okay, thanks."

Andrew and Steven waited.

"That was my man. He says the abductors are heading northeast. We might just want to pay a visit to the Crow's Nest."

— — — — — — — — — — — — — — — —

Abby sat sandwiched between Neil and Kurt in the back of a black SUV and thought ironically that all the heroines she had read about escaping from vehicles must have borrowed some fairy dust.

They most certainly hadn't been hemmed in on both sides by the likes of these two ruffians. Neil was over six-feet tall, and Kurt's robust, burly build blocked any hope of escaping from the other side.

With a sigh, she watched as the vehicle sped by shorelines lined with coconut trees. Only occasionally did they even pass another vehicle, tightening the knot in her stomach that no one would find her out here.

She had hoped someone would recognize her at the bar. She had even thought about trying to cry for help or making a run for it, but Neil had dashed such hopes by a warning look and tightening his grip on her arm.

Neil's cell phone chirped, breaking the icy silence. "We're almost there," he replied. "Yes, we've got the girl. No, everything is going like clockwork. Really? Well now, that is good news. Okay, we'll see you in a few."

He flipped his phone closed and looked intently at Abby. "Well, my dear, another guest will be joining us."

Abby chose to ignore him, staring out the front window. But something in his voice gave her a chill.

"You'll never guess, so I'll tell you. It's your dear Uncle Rick."

She couldn't hide the horror she felt. "It can't be true," she said.

"Come now, would I lie to you?" he laughed mockingly.

"Never, I'm sure," Abby retorted and turned to face him. "Like you'd never lie to your cousin or grandfather."

Neil laughed. "Kurt, would you get a load of this!"

Kurt snorted. "Yeah, she's breaking my heart."

Abby clenched her fists and felt them grow clammy. She felt it was impossible for Rick to have been captured as well, and yet, she felt afraid for him. These men would stop at nothing to get what they wanted.

Without warning, Neil reached around her shoulder, pulling her into his chest and blinding her with a dark, thick cloth. She tried elbowing him in the stomach, but he was too quick for her.

She shoved him away and reached to remove the blindfold but felt Kurt grab her hands, binding them with another piece of fabric.

"Why don't you just hog-tie and gag me while you're at it," she snapped, managing to pull away from Kurt's rough grasp.

"Tempting, but unnecessary," Neil laughed. "But Kurt has done a sloppy job tying your hands, so you must promise to behave – or I'll have to tighten them myself."

"She won't keep still," Kurt muttered, reaching to tie them tighter himself. Abby pushed herself firmly back into her seat to keep him from reaching her bound hands. Kurt swore and shoved her over, causing her to fall back into Neil.

Hot tears stung her eyes as Kurt tightened the coarse cloth, and she felt Neil grab her shoulders to prop her back against the middle seat.

She bit her tongue and determined not to say anything else. She supposed the reason for her treatment was that they were nearing their destination, and her captors did not want her to see the way. What reason they had to fear her escape, she couldn't guess.

Kurt and Neil were making jokes at her expense, but she tuned them out and started to focus on any verse that came to mind. "Only be thou strong and very courageous ..." Joshua's words from the Old Testament spoke to her heart. She couldn't let these bullies get the best of her.

"The battle belongs to the Lord," she thought as fragments of Scripture came to mind. "It's not by might nor by power ..."

"Here we are," Kurt said as the vehicle came to a halt. He reached for Abby and yanked her out of the vehicle. She staggered along what seemed to be a stone walkway and up some short steps.

She heard a door open and a mixture of voices. Suddenly, she heard a woman's voice say, "I see you've had your fun, but I don't think these are necessary any more." Soft, but certainly not kind, hands removed her blindfold, and Abby blinked to adjust to the bright sun as Kurt reluctantly released her hands.

The voice was so familiar, but it took a moment for her eyes to focus. "Edith Brightly," Abby said, not believing her eyes.

"I don't know why Neil seems so impressed with your skills," she mocked, escorting Abby inside what seemed to be a mansion. "For one, your reports were always lacking.

"And for two, you never saw this coming, did you?"

Abby didn't reply, trying to take in the scene. They were now inside a large hall and through the sliding doors beyond, she could see the ocean's water shimmering in the sun.

A man approached them, whom she recognized as Ralston. He addressed Brightly, "Mr. Zarchoff has requested to see you and DeWitt immediately."

"I'll deal with you later," she promised and turned to Neil. "It's always a pleasure to have good news for the boss."

"When will Benton be arriving?" Neil asked.

"Soon," Brightly turned and walked away.

"I'll be just a minute," Neil said.

"So this is the girl," Ralston said, indicating Abby, who was being watched closely by Kurt. "The guest room is ready."

At that moment, an armed guard appeared and said quickly, "The Russians have just arrived."

"They're early," Neil muttered. "Ralston, you and Kurt go escort them to the lounge. I have to go join Brightly."

"What about her?" Kurt asked.

"Have the guard put her in the room," Neil said and hurried away.

Kurt and Ralston disappeared in the opposite direction, and Abby cringed as the guard reached for her arm.

"This way," he said, clearly impatient. He nearly dragged her up a flight of stairs where two other guards met him.

"Why aren't you at your post?" one of them demanded.

"The Russians have arrived, and I was told to report to Ralston."

"What are you doing with her? We're supposed to supervise the delivery of the last briefcase."

"Just get rid of her, or we're going to be late," the other added.

"I was told to put her in the guest room," he said. "What is that supposed to mean?"

"It's on the other side of the house," the first said and reached for the handle of a nearby room. "Put her in here for now."

The man swung the door open, and another shoved Abby inside, locking the door firmly behind her.

She heard them talking as they hurried away. "We've got to alert the escort that the Russians are ahead of schedule. Their yacht arrived moments ago …"

Their voices faded away, and Abby started to look at her surroundings. She felt a ray of hope as she noticed the window wasn't barred, and the room was actually quite inviting. The guard must have put her in this room by mistake. Whatever Ralston meant by "the guest room," she was sure this wasn't what he had in mind.

Chapter 16

The Moment to Decide

If the guards had a made a mistake, it wouldn't be too long before someone found out. Abby ran to the window and looked at her options. She could easily pop the screens and climb out, but she was on the second story.

The room looked out toward some open lawn that disappeared into a forest of palm trees and shrubs. No one was in sight.

She rushed over to the closet to see if there was anything she could use. There was an assortment of shoes and clothes, ranging from party dresses to suits, from swimsuits to overalls. She grabbed the overalls and a baseball cap. They were a drab color and would certainly not call as much attention to herself as the yellow sundress she was wearing.

Of course, they were several sizes too big, but Abby slipped them over her dress anyway and tucked her hair up inside the hat.

She quickly finished her search of the closet and turned to look under the bed. There were several old suitcases, a duffle bag and a briefcase.

"Briefcase," she thought, remembering something the guards had said. She clutched it on a whim and tossed it over to the window.

But there was nothing to use to climb out. Frowning, Abby looked at the bed. Perhaps she could use sheets?

She flung off the comforter and started peeling away the crème-colored sheets, knotting them together. She tied one end around the base of the thick wooden bed frame and carried the remaining heap to the window.

She peered out and saw no one. As quickly as possible, she opened the windows, removed the screen, tossed out the briefcase behind the bushes below and let down her sheets.

It was now or never, so Abby backed out the window and climbed down as far as she could before jumping. She landed in the dirt behind the shrub bushes and thanks to her long overalls, avoided scratches on her legs.

The crème sheets hanging out the window stood out like a warning flag, and she knew she needed to hurry before someone noticed.

In a hunched position, she moved along the perimeter of the house until the window was out of sight.

She needed to get away from the house and into the woods. From there, she would just need to find the shoreline or the road and try to make her way to a city or somewhere she could get help.

But the manicured lawn looked like an eternity wide, and she doubted very much she could cross it undetected.

Just then, she heard two men's voices very close by. A loud noise followed, and Abby realized it was the sound of a hedge trimmer.

The noise grew closer, and she tried to backtrack, but the hedges started to thin. She crouched as low as she could, holding her breath.

The hedge trimmer stopped and a man with a thick Bahamian accent muttered, "What the ..."

Knowing she had been detected, Abby bolted from her hiding place and started for the woods. She felt the man must be right on her heels. She had just reached a large shed when she tripped and fell to the ground, the man seemingly on top of her.

Blindly, she tried scratching him with her nails, but the man had her arms pinned in no time.

"Abby, Abby," the man said in a firm but kind voice. "It's all right, calm down."

For the first time, Abby caught a glimpse of his face. Though disguised, she recognized him as none other than Coby Ward.

He released his grip, and she quickly brushed herself off. "You scared me to death," she scolded.

"Well, I wasn't expecting to find you behind the hedges either," he replied, grinning. "How did you manage that get-up?" He looked at her oversized trousers and chuckled.

Abby related her story, and Coby's smile quickly vanished. "And, they have Rick – or that's what Neil told me. And Edith Brightly is here, and she is a traitor. And the Russians have arrived to pick up the last shipment."

"Whoa, slow down," Coby said. "So Rick was right about Brightly. Did you see Rick by any chance?"

"No, I'm not sure if he's here yet," Abby said. "How did you manage to get undercover?"

"Never mind that now," Coby said. "We've got to get you out of here before someone discovers you're missing."

"What about the Russians? They're going to get away if we don't do something."

"I promised Rick that if I found you, I'd get you somewhere safe," Coby said firmly.

"But the whole point of our being here is to stop the shipment of PS59," Abby insisted. "We're the only ones who have a chance of doing that."

Coby sighed, "What do you propose? That you and I march in there and arrest everyone?"

"I heard some guards say they were to supervise the delivery of the last briefcase," Abby said. "I'm guessing that they are disguising the shipment by hiding it in a briefcase."

"And where is this briefcase?" Coby asked, still not convinced.

"They were going to take it to the Russian's yacht," she said, looking toward the water. "There are three yachts there now; it must be one of them."

"There was a briefcase in the bushes where I was trimming," Coby said thoughtfully. "I wonder if we could use that."

"I found that in the room the guards locked me inside," Abby said. "It was a wild idea, but I was thinking maybe we could substitute it for the real one."

"You're right about one thing," Coby said. "This is a wild idea. But it could work." He moved toward a golf cart parked beside the shed and tossed her a pair of loppers.

"We can make our way toward the yacht by acting like grounds workers. I've got a clearance pass, so if anyone questions us, I'll show him that. Whatever happens, don't look anyone directly in the face." He chuckled. "You don't look anything like a Bahamian landscaper."

Abby grinned as she hopped inside the golf cart. After retrieving the briefcase as carefully as possible, she hid it underneath some palm branches until they reached the outer property by the beach.

Coby jumped out of the cart and started trimming the hedges. Abby grabbed a black plastic bag and followed him. The two worked in silence, but both watched the yacht out of the corner of their eye.

Finally, a group of men emerged from the closest yacht. Some were clearly El GATO guards, while the other three appeared to be foreigners. Two of the foreigners remained behind, while the group headed back toward the mansion.

When they were out of earshot, Coby and Abby moved back toward the golf cart.

"It's now or never," he whispered. "Do you have the briefcase?"

"Yes," Abby said. "What's your plan?"

Coby pulled off his watch. "I'm going to board the yacht with the story one of the men dropped this. I'll take care of the guards. You sneak on board with the fake briefcase and try to find the real one.

"We won't have much time. The rest of the Russians will be back soon. They're probably just paying up right now."

Abby nodded and watched as Coby walked toward the yacht and boarded. She faintly heard him mention his watch before he and the guards disappeared out of sight.

With a furtive glance back at the main house, Abby emerged from behind the cart and boarded the yacht when she thought no one was looking.

Throwing caution to the wind, she hurried below deck and entered an elaborate lounge, complete with wide screen TV and bar. Her heart started to race. How would she ever find the briefcase?

Just then, she spotted it. Relieved beyond words that it was not locked in some secret closet or inside a safe, she hurried over.

The suitcase was black, and hers was a dark brown, but she didn't care. The black case was closed but not locked. She quickly popped it open to see small bricks neatly lined in rows. The sweet smell that flooded her nostrils told her she had the right briefcase.

Closing it quickly and feeling as though she had been in the lounge for far too long, she cautiously approached the stairs. She did not hear any voices and assumed that Coby must be "taking care" of the guards, as he put it.

Just as she reached the top step, a man's voice shouted out. She raised her head and saw one of El GATO's guards pointing at the yacht and yelling in a loud voice.

Had he seen Coby, or had he seen her? Abby didn't have time to guess, so she ran toward the exit.

But it was too late. The guard and several others had nearly reached the yacht. They would intercept her if she tried to leave the way she came.

She rushed toward the back of the yacht. She saw no other choice. Abby flinched and jumped overboard, briefcase in hand.

The impact of the splash awakened her to a new problem. Her overalls made her feel as though she were swimming inside a sleeping bag, and then the zipper was stuck. She had to let go of the briefcase if she were to keep from drowning.

"Better at the bottom of the ocean than in their hands," she sputtered and made for the shore as it sank beneath her.

It was a losing battle, and Abby knew it. By the time she reached the shore, she was gasping for breath – and surrounded by more than a dozen guards.

—————————————————

"Thank goodness for four-wheel drive," thought Garth as he sped over potholes and uneven pavement.

The mood inside the jeep was tense, to say the least. Just minutes ago, Garth had received two phone calls, the first from a correspondent who had been shadowing the suspected Russian clients since the time they first checked into the Atlantis Resort on Paradise Island.

His report indicated that the Russians had been spotted earlier that morning on a flight to Cat Island. After landing at the Arthur's Town airport at the north end of the island, they had headed southeast, which seemed to match up with the Crow's Nest theory.

The second call had been from his man who was trailing Rick. His news was even more disheartening. The men who had abducted Rick were paid criminals who had been eluding justice for some time. They were last spotted traveling northwest, just five miles south of the Crow's Nest location.

Everything indicated that Garth, Steven and Andrew were heading in the right direction. Garth had called his connections at the Bahamian Coast Guard, and a team was on its way. Air support was scheduled to be half an hour behind.

None of the three spoke a word after the last phone call. There was nothing left to say, and no one wanted to voice the fear that was gnawing inside each of them.

Yes, they would find Rick and Abby, but would they find them in time?

_ _ _ _ _ _ _ _ _ _ _ _ _ _ _

Abby tried not to flinch as Kurt stepped forward from the group surrounding her, reached for the cap that disguised her face and yanked it off, revealing her curly brown hair.

"You," he sputtered, cursing under his breath. "What is going on here?"

Abby remained silent, and one of the Russian's guards staggered toward Kurt to answer. "I was keeping watch. I felt a shooting pain in my head, and then I don't remember anything." He glanced at Abby in confusion. The Russian guard was a sturdily built man standing six-feet tall. He looked doubtfully at the petite woman standing in front of him.

"Who is your accomplice?" Kurt demanded.

When Abby did not reply, he reached for her arm, but she moved away just in time, stepping back into the shallows of the water.

"No one was with me. I was trying to escape. That's all," she said.

Two of the guards moved in, each taking her by the arm. Kurt turned toward the house, and the men marched her after him.

She was still dripping wet when they reentered the mansion. They ascended a stairway and wound through the hallways until Abby wasn't sure she could remember her way back. Finally, they reached a black door. Kurt opened it, and Abby could barely discern several figures in the dim interior.

"I have another guest to announce," Kurt sneered. "Miss Abigail Grant, please step forward."

The guards shoved her inside the windowless room. The interior was painted a dismal gray, and the furniture consisted of three metal chairs, a square table and an old ugly lamp.

"Abby!" a hoarse voice whispered, and she turned to see her Uncle Rick, slouched in one of the chairs.

"Rick!" she replied and started toward him, but a broadly built man stepped in front of her path. She stared up into a pair of dark, expressionless eyes and staggered backward. The hint of a smile tugged at the corners of his lips as he reached for her hands.

"Miss Grant, I am pleased for you to join us."

The coldness of his voice, thickly laden with a Russian accent, sent chills through her. His large hands grasped her small ones firmly, and she could not withdraw them.

"But my dear, you are shivering."

Abby managed to look away from his abysmal stare and glanced back to Rick. His eyes held an emotion she had never before seen her uncle express: fear.

"Do sit down," the man's abstract voice continued as he backed her into a chair. "Now why are you trembling so?"

"She went for a swim," Kurt interrupted.

"I did not address the question to you," the man coldly replied. Kurt backed away as if a snake had struck him.

"Miss Grant, I asked you a question."

"I did go for a swim. And the house is cold, so that is why I am trembling." Abby barely recognized her own voice.

The man did smile at her. But it was the most heartless smile she had ever seen. He turned away to reach for a glass of wine before he continued to question her.

"Would you like some wine?"

"No thank you," Abby replied quickly.

"Then I hope you don't mind if I do."

"Of course not."

"Then let us get back to business. Why did you go for a swim?"

"I did not want to impose on your hospitality any longer, so I thought I would make my leave."

He actually laughed. It sounded like a crackle deep inside his throat. "Forgive me. You are more spirited than I had anticipated."

He turned to Kurt. "What have you to say? Why did you interrupt this young lady's swim?"

"She was on the Russian's yacht. I don't know what she was doing there. Someone saw her, and she jumped overboard. That's when we captured her. One of the Russian guards was clubbed over the head. He's a pretty hefty fellow. I asked her if she were alone, and she said yes. I couldn't get any more out of her, and then I brought her here."

The gentlemanly façade on the Russian man's face disappeared. The reference to his client's yacht made him narrow his eyes.

"What were you doing on the yacht?" he asked quietly. Abby could sense the danger behind his voice.

"I wanted to get away. I did not know whose yacht it was."

"Surely you could not take out a guard all by yourself."

"Two guards, actually," Kurt added.

The man stared at her, waiting for an answer.

"It was just a matter of leverage, really," Abby said, moistening her lip.

The man walked over to her, his eyes never leaving her face. He put a hand on her shoulder.

"A matter of leverage," he repeated.

Suddenly, he grabbed her arm and twisted it. Abby winced in pain and bit her tongue.

"Who helped you?"

"There was no one," she gasped.

"Leave her alone," Rick cried, leaping out of his chair. It took three guards to control him.

At that moment, the door burst open. Abby could see Ralston silhouetted against the doorway. For a second, he looked at her. The next instant, he turned to the man beside her.

He cleared his throat and began, "I'm sorry to interrupt, Mr. Zarchoff, but there's been a breach in security."

"Zarchoff!" Abby thought to herself. To her relief, he released her arm and turned his full attention to Ralston.

"The Russians claim the briefcase we delivered contained tools, of all things," Ralston said.

"Tools?" Zarchoff asked.

"Something to the effect of a pair of loppers, hammers, wrenches ..."

"I personally inspected the briefcase myself," Zarchoff said. "I showed it to our Russian clients before making the exchange. There must be a mistake."

"I saw the briefcase as well, Sir. The briefcase the Russians now have is slightly different in color. The Russians are claiming we made a dishonest swap while they shared a drink with you."

"Tell them we are extremely sorry for the inconvenience and that there must be an honest mistake somewhere. Give them their payment back for security, and tell them we will get to the bottom of this in no time," Zarchoff replied coolly. "We can't risk losing their trust."

"Right away, Sir," Ralston said and disappeared.

Zarchoff whirled to face Abby, who was trying very hard not to look him in the face. She knew she could not hold a bluff for long.

"It was you, wasn't it?" he demanded. "You were doing more than merely trying to escape, weren't you?"

"I don't know what you are talking about," she said.

"No more games, Miss Grant. Tell me what I want to know, or I will make you tell me."

Once more, he reached for her, but this time, Abby expected his move. She jumped from the chair and rushed toward the door. Only two guards remained who ran to intercept her, but she cleared the entrance – only to crash into the chest of Neil DeWitt.

The impact sent them both to the floor, but Neil quickly gained the upper hand, grabbing her arms. She managed to kick him twice in the shins before he had her on her feet and pinned.

"Let me go," she muttered, elbowing him in the ribs.

"You really should stop running into me," he said, tightening his grip and forcing her back into the room.

"You're heartless," she muttered at last as he thrust her down into the steel chair and started tying her to it.

He chuckled bitterly. It sounded like something Susan would say.

"Perfect timing, Neil," Zarchoff said. "How are our clients?"

"That's what I was coming to tell you," Neil said, turning away from Abby. "They've left with their security."

"What!"

"They spotted the Coast Guard and thought this was a trap."

"The Coast Guard!"

"It's confirmed," another guard appeared, breathless. "The Coast Guard is coming. We're discovered."

Zarchoff swore. He turned to Neil. "Enact Plan Z. Twenty minutes."

"What about the prisoners?" Neil asked.

"We'll leave them here and lock the door. Their friends will never find them."

Abby's palms sweated. What did that mean?

Zarchoff turned to her and tightly cupped her chin in his large, thick hands. "Well done, Miss Grant. But I'm afraid your victory is short-lived. You see, this building is wired with C4 explosives. In twenty minutes, everything will go up in smoke."

He turned and barked some final orders at the guards and disappeared. Neil started to follow him.

"Neil! Don't do this," Abby said.

"What's this? A pitiful cry for mercy? Really, Abby, you're stooping rather low."

"Think of Duff and Dixie."

"I'll give them your best," he sneered.

"Think of Susan."

"She is dead to me," he said coldly, "as you will be shortly."

"There are two kinds of deaths, Neil. You can kill the body but not the soul."

"Detective turned missionary, is that what you are?" he scoffed. "I'm wasting my breath."

"No, you're wasting your life," Abby retorted as he slammed the door behind him … and turned the lock.

For a moment, neither Rick nor Abby said anything. The sound of the door shutting seemed so final. Even if there had been a way of escape, both Uncle and Niece were firmly tied to the hard chairs.

Rick managed to slide himself closer to Abby so he could see her profile. A tear was sliding down her cheek.

"Don't cry, Abby," he said, but his voice sounded empty.

"I'm not crying for myself," she said. "It's that I was thinking, Neil has no hope …"

"Don't waste your tears on that scumbag," he spat.

"… You have no hope," Abby said. "You're not a prisoner because of these ropes or the locked door.

You're a captive by your own choice. I'm going to be home with my Savior in less than twenty minutes, Uncle. Where will you be?"

Rick was silent. Did he really belong in the same sentence as the man who just locked the door behind him? Surely he had never committed the same crimes as Neil had. He had been a good person, give or take.

"So you think I've wasted my life, just like that fellow?" Rick asked, surprised at the bitter sound of his voice.

Abby paused. "Only what's done for Christ will last."

"Stop quoting me riddles," he snapped but secretly felt ashamed. He knew what Abby meant. Her mother and he had learned the same verses in Sunday school together. He could quote them just as well as she could. He had just never believed.

"Rick, it's not about being perfect," Abby said gently. "I've made enough mistakes in my eighteen years to make me thankful for God's grace. He gave us something we didn't deserve when he sent his Son to die for the sins of the world – for you and me.

"I have less than twenty minutes, Abby," Rick said. "There's no chance for me to make up for lost time."

"Yes there is, Rick," Abby protested. "All you have to do is accept God's gift of salvation. Ask him to forgive you of your sins. Thank him for dying for you. It doesn't take more than a few seconds to talk to him. Believe that he wants to save you, and he will."

"It would be nice if he would unbolt that door," Rick sighed.

"That would be nice," Abby agreed, "but in terms of eternity, that door is not going to make much of a difference."

"Is that what you meant when you said there are two kinds of deaths?" Rick asked.

"Yes," Abby sighed, thinking back to her last words with Neil. "If you die today knowing Christ and if Neil lives for a few more dozen years before dying without knowing Him, I'd rather be you today than him tomorrow."

"I should never have asked you to come," Rick muttered. "Your mother will never forgive me."

"I wanted to come," Abby said. "It's more my fault that I'm here than it is yours. I could have slipped away, but instead, I wanted to be a hero and stop that shipment."

"Did you do that all by yourself?" he asked.

"No, Coby was with me. I just hope he got away."

"I thought the story of you taking out two guards was a little sketchy," he grinned, but then sighed.

"Your mother. . ." Rick repeated thoughtfully, "She's been hounding me with the same salvation stuff for as long as I can remember. It was Jane's death that really turned me away from it all. And now, Michelle will be losing you."

The thought sent a pang through Abby, but she knew her mom's faith was deep. "I know Mom will forgive you, because Jesus has forgiven us. We are to forgive as well."

Rick took in a deep breath and blew it out.

Abby's thoughts turned back toward home. Her mother and dad had always been there for her. Her friends ... Andrew. She swallowed a lump in her throat, wishing she could take back her words from their last argument. He had been right, of course, but she just did not want to admit it.

Andrew had learned something she had not been willing to accept, that God does not care if you are a governor or a garbage man, He just wants you to be faithful to Him in your every day tasks.

Rick interrupted her thoughts. "I thought on what you said, Abby, and..." Rick began hesitantly.

"And I believe, Abby; I believe."

Abby started to sob.

"What are you crying for now?" Rick asked hoarsely.

"I'm so happy," Abby said, the tears freely flowing down her cheeks. "Maybe we don't have more than a few minutes to live, but I've never been happier."

Chapter 17

The Countdown

The jeep had long since left the beaten path, and Garth was now maneuvering potholes and tree roots on a narrow dirt road.

"Look out!" Steven cried, and Garth sharply yanked the wheel to avoid colliding with another vehicle.

"That guy was flying," Andrew frowned. "He had to be going over fifty."

"I think we're getting close," Garth said.

At that moment, two more vehicles appeared, going equally as fast as the first.

"Something is wrong," Garth thought to himself. Both vehicles were crammed full of uniformed men.

A fourth less distinguished vehicle appeared. It was a small, rusty red car, packed full of Bahamian men. To avoid hitting the jeep, they colliding with some shrub trees and became stuck in the mud.

Andrew watched in disbelief as they scrambled out of the car and started running.

One of the men had obviously been slightly injured in the crash, for he remained behind to hobble along by himself.

Garth slammed on the breaks, obstructing his path. The man swore and glared at Garth.

"What gives?" the man scowled, trying to work his way around the vehicle.

"Is this the way to the Crow's Nest?" Garth asked.

"You're crazy if you want to go there," the man said.

"I don't understand," Garth said.

"The place is going to explode in twenty minutes," the man said and turned to hurry away. "If I were you, I would get out of here!"

"What does that mean?" Andrew asked.

"I believe the man was literally telling the truth," Garth said and shifted into gear. "Something is wrong at the Crow's Nest. If it's going to explode, as the man said, in twenty minutes, we don't have much time to find our friends."

A moment later, the large estate appeared in view, and Garth hid the jeep behind some low-lying trees.

The scene was chaotic. Jeeps and trucks of all sizes were speeding from the property, and a lone helicopter had landed on the open grass. Uniformed men and civilians were running from the mansion, some simply fleeing into the woods as if for their lives.

"We go on foot from here," Garth said.

"How do you expect us to get in there?" Andrew asked.

"This place is in an uproar. Be as inconspicuous as possible, and I doubt anyone will notice you. All the same, take this," Garth said and handed each a handgun. "I hope you won't need it."

"We should synchronize our watches," Steven suggested. "That man said twenty minutes back there. If that's what someone told him, we'd better plan on ten minutes."

"Good point," Garth said. "Meet back here in ten minutes. If we haven't found Rick and Abby by then, we probably aren't going to."

Andrew started to protest, but Garth cut him off. "Let's not argue; let's get going."

The three hugged the tree line until they reached the mansion. They could hear what sounded like an alarm, and its pitch seemed to send everyone around them into panic.

The trio helped themselves to a back door and found the corresponding kitchen to be empty.

"This place is like a ghost town," Garth muttered. "We may have less time than the man told us. If we're going to cover this place, we've got to split up."

"Ten minutes," he called over his shoulder as he took off running in one direction.

"I say we stay together," Steven said to Andrew. "Come on." The two took off for a flight of stairs. Each friend took one side of the hallway to do a quick scan of the rooms. The hallway seemed to wind for an eternity, and the two were painfully conscious they didn't have much time left to search.

"We've got two minutes, Steve," Andrew said.

"Keep going," his friend replied. "We have to finish this hallway."

"Hey, this door is locked," Andrew said, twisting the handle. "Is there anyone in there?"

A muffled sound reached his ears. "I think I hear someone," he said.

"On the count of the three," Steven said, and together, they broke down the door.

It took a moment for their eyes to adjust to the dim interior.

"Steve! Andrew!" Abby cried.

"This place is going to explode any minute now," Rick said. "It's rigged with C4."

Steven and Andrew quickly untied them from the steel chairs, and they rushed for the door.

"Follow me," Steven cried, and the four raced through the hall and down the stairs. There was no sight of Garth – or anyone else for that matter. The estate was eerily empty.

They cleared the back door and ran for the trees. The alarm was now a high-pitched scream. Steven knew they would not reach the jeep in time.

Abby tripped over some roots and fell into what seemed to be a drainage ditch. It was behind a canopy of trees.

"Everybody down!" Steven said, and the rest jumped into the ditch. An ear-splitting boom rocked the island, and the immaculate estate behind them exploded into burning rubble.

After the blast, the four cautiously peeked over the edge of the ditch. What remained of the estate was consumed with flames. The sound of sirens once more reached their ears, but it was not the same shrill alarm. It was coming from the direction of the ocean.

"It sounds like the Coast Guard. Come on, let's see if Garth is at the jeep," Steven said, brushing himself off and climbing out of the ditch.

Andrew offered Abby a hand, and Abby replied with a hug.

"What was that for?" he grinned.

"I'm so glad to see you – I didn't think I'd get to see you again," she said. "I'm so sorry for what I said before."

"I'm sorry too," he said and for the first time, had a chance to get a good look at his friend. "But you're all wet! And why in the world are you wearing over-sized coveralls?"

Abby glanced down at the soiled and damp coveralls and looked at Rick. He laughed as she attempted to get out of them without tripping.

"She has some wild stories to tell you," Rick said with a twinkle in his eye.

The sound of the sirens grew louder, and they could now see several craft on the beach.

"We should notify them of what is going on," Rick said to Steve.

"You go ahead," Steven said. "I've got to see if Garth is waiting for us at the jeep."

"Garth Owens?" Rick asked with a frown.

"Yes, he helped us find this place," Steven said. "It sounds like he was double-crossed by Brightly and determined to find out what was going on."

Rick sighed with relief. "I'm glad to hear that. I thought he might have been the insider. But I still don't understand what you two are doing here."

"It's a long story," Andrew said.

"Then we'll save it for later," Rick said. "We still need to clear up a couple things."

"We'll meet you at the beach," Steven called back to him over his shoulder.

"I'm going with Steve," Andrew said to Abby. "Can I leave you with Rick without you getting yourself into more trouble?"

"I promise to try to behave," she said and hurried after Rick.

As they neared the beach, Abby was surprised to see the Russian yacht next to the Coast Guard vessels.

"Rick, that's the yacht the Russian clients were using!" she whispered in excitement.

"And look, there's Coby!" he cried. The Bahamian giant caught sight of his old friend and ran to greet him.

"Thank goodness you're both safe," he said, embracing his friend. "We've got some good and bad news."

"Then start with the good news," Rick said. "I need to hear something good has come out of all this."

Coby began to relate his story. After Abby was captured, he escaped from the yacht and phoned the Coast Guard, who were already on their way, thanks to a tip from Garth. They managed to intercept the fleeing Russian yacht and were transporting its occupants for safeguarding until further questioning.

Ground support had also intercepted several fleeing occupants from the estate, including Edith Brightly.

"Between the Russians and Brightly, we should be able to piece together the missing pieces," Coby said.

"What's the bad news?" Abby asked.

Coby looked at her with a sad smile. "I'm afraid Zarchoff, DeWitt, Ralston and even the man named Kurt all managed to escape. The Coast Guard is still searching, and the airports have been warned about them. But someone rumored there was a private helicopter used in their escape. My instincts tell me they got just far enough away to bed down in a secluded location until everything quiets down.

"The other bit of bad news is that we think someone escaped with the shipment of PS59," he said. "We need that evidence to hold the Russians, and their yacht is clean. Abby, whatever happened to that briefcase?"

Abby's face brightened. "El GATO didn't get away with the briefcase, and neither did the Russians. If you'll search the shallows by the boats, you'll find the briefcase. I took it overboard with me when I jumped off the yacht to try to escape. It's somewhere at the bottom."

"We'll get a scuba crew to find it right away," Coby said and called over several men. As they hurried away, he turned his attention back to Rick and Abby.

"But how in the world did you escape? It must have been some stroke of pure luck, because this place was swarming with guards."

Rick looked at Abby and smiled. "No, Coby, if there's one thing I've learned, it's that this whole adventure – if you care to call it that – has had absolutely nothing to do with luck."

Chapter 18

The Greatest Adventure

"They're here!" Freddy announced and hurried outside. At the sound, Abby descended the stairs and met her uncle, Garth, Coby and several of his brothers in the Ward's living room. She was wearing a denim skirt and flowered peasant top, and her face was all smiles.

It seemed like years had passed since the adventure of yesterday. Garth was relieved beyond words when Steven and Andrew had finally reached the jeep. The trio had driven to the beach to meet up with Rick and Abby not long afterward.

The scuba team had met with success in their quest, and the briefcase had proven relatively water-tight. Only a few of the PS59 bricks had been damaged; most had been wrapped securely enough to keep out the ocean water.

To most, the recovery of the long-rumored psycho-stimulant was the biggest success story of the day. Not only did they have it as evidence, but now the DEA could better research the formula and the expected result of the drug. Both the Russians and Brightly had so far proven tight-lipped, but the DEA and its partners were convinced they could come up with a deal that would make both parties much more cooperative.

Abby's biggest disappointment was that Neil had gotten away. Garth had assured her his men were doing their best to find him, but Abby had a sinking feeling that she had not seen the last of him yet.

But she pushed the thought aside for the evening. Tonight was a celebration, and the Ward clan had invited Steve, Andrew, as well as the other *Wings of the Dawn* crew, to join them for a festive dinner.

Garth had arrived early to discuss a couple last-minute details with Coby and Rick, and now, he smiled at her as she waited for the very eager Freddy to usher in her brothers and friends.

"Abby!" Amber greeted her with hugs. "We were so worried about you."

"But we knew God was watching over you," Kim added.

"He certainly was," Abby replied and winked at Rick. So far, he hadn't had a chance to tell anyone else his wonderful news, which in her estimation, far surpassed any of yesterday's discoveries.

Jimmy and Matt were soon at the sisters' sides, and Abby noted with interest that Jimmy gently reached for Kim's hand. Kim's eyes twinkled, and Abby knew she had her own story to share with her later.

"You certainly have a nice bunch of friends," Garth said, walking over to her side.

"Yes, but that's not all of them," Abby said and peeked out the window to where she could see Freddy engaging Andrew in some new argument.

"You know, I never did have a chance to say thank you," she said, turning back to the agent.

"For what?"

"For coming to find us," she said.

"You had a lot of us worried," he smiled. "But I think many of us – especially El GATO – underestimated your abilities. You have the creativity and simple ingenuity that a lot of agents would do well to remember."

"If you want to call my makeshift solutions a mark of ingenuity, go right ahead," she laughed. The agent's face warmed into a handsome smile, and she once again thought of Dixie. How much she had to tell her friend!

Steven and Andrew finally entered, and Garth greeted them with firm handshakes. Andrew's eyes sparkled when they met her own, but momentarily clouded. Garth and Steven walked toward the Ward's large dining room as he lagged behind.

"What is it, Andrew?" she asked. "Aren't you glad to see me again?"

"How long have you and Garth known each other?" he asked.

"Oh, he's been helping Rick with the case since I started," she said. "I met him back in Belmont Springs."

Andrew grew quiet. "Don't tell me you're jealous!" Abby teased.

"Of course not," he protested.

"He is rather good looking," Abby said slyly. "But then, I'm afraid he doesn't quite have your sense of humor."

"Maybe you just need to get to know him better," Andrew played along.

"Maybe," Abby shrugged and walked toward the dining room. "But I think I happen to prefer airplane mechanics to secret agents."

At that moment, Mrs. Ward appeared, bustling about with final meal preparations, while everyone gathered around the table.

Freddy quickly claimed a place next to Abby and across from Andrew. Jimmy asked if he might thank God for everyone's safety and for the delicious meal, and Coby nodded.

"Dear Father, thank you for your watchful care for us this week. Thank you for reminding us that nothing is impossible with you. You made a retired airplane come back to life to meet a delivery deadline, protected our family and friends against the well-devised plans of their enemies, and used the arson of a church building to bring together a church family. You are the God who uses weak vessels to overcome the strong and the seemingly foolish to confound the earthly wisdom of men. Thank you for the loving hands that have prepared this food, and please bless our time together. Amen."

"Amen," Rick whispered and looked up at Abby. No longer did he despise her faith; he now shared with her in it. His heart felt warmer than it had in years.

Abby looked at Jimmy. "I still can't believe you actually got *Wings* to fly again."

Andrew grinned, "Let's just say you are never too dented or too dusty a vessel for God to use you."

"There he goes, personifying that plane again," Matt laughed at his brother, who ignored him and retold the story of *Wings* flying to the Bahamas to assist the Brown's church.

"Where exactly is that?" Freddy asked, helping himself to a generous portion of his mom's cooking.

"Do you remember a yellow building next to the old library?" Matt asked. "The new church building will be just down the road from there."

"Oh yeah, that's not too far from here," Freddy said.

"You should check it out some time," Jimmy said. "There are plenty of youth like yourself. Several were helping me with the construction yesterday."

The conversation turned to other things, and Abby drifted off into her own thoughts. Tomorrow, she would be going home, and leaving behind her new friends the Wards and the action-packed events of the last week. But she felt ready to leave and to her own surprise, eager to help out at the mission next week, since Rick had told her she could have some time off.

"She's more of a sidekick than I bargained for," she heard Rick saying. She looked up at him as he continued with a new light in his eyes, "We had the adventure of a lifetime."

Abby couldn't agree more.

LaVergne, TN USA
16 December 2010
209033LV00001B/1/P